The Dragon Cycles

by Alan Gold

For Beatrix

Chapter 1

Dragons in the Valley

There weren't always dragons in the Valley. But this noon, their wings blotted out the sun.

Shankon spat in the dim light. "What's the difference between a dragon's wing and a bellows?" is how he framed the riddle.

Granger the Younger screwed up his face at the old man. "I don't know."

"The bellows doesn't leave the stink of monster crotch behind." He spat again, with scant production. "We're in for a time of it tonight."

Granger opened his mouth, closed it again, and looked out across the shadows that rippled over the valley like the waves of a dark ocean.

"You always said the worst thing about a dragon was it would cook you too much before it ate you."

"And that is so, with a single dragon. An inn with a dragon in the kitchen would be a lonely place. There's no custom for a meal of coal." Shankon shook his head at the sadness of it all.

"But ten thousand beasts like these?" His arm swept across the dark, noon sky and he raised his voice above the torrent of the wings. "They'll poison our fields with their foul issue. Our crops will wither and the ground will turn to ash."

Shankon cocked an eyebrow at the lad. "Do you know what gunpowder is?"

Granger shook his head, a little embarrassed.

"The cannons we saw on Arvon's Day? Gunpowder gave them their voice."

Granger had loved Arvon's Day. The flutter of the high pennants, yellow, green and blue in the wind. The sharp aftertaste of the hunks of meat, still hot from the oaken smoke of the pit and wolfed down from wooden skewers. The spectacle of the horsemen. The tinkling voices of girls not much older than himself, whose allure transcended their age. Even the worn-out speeches delivered by pompous old men from balconies carried a soothing rhythm that lasted long after the words were lost in the wind.

But the thundering cannons had anchored Arvon's Day in his mind.

"Remember the cannons?" Shankon would ask.

"I loved the cannons," Granger would respond. "I surely did."

"Never forget them," Shankon would conclude. "We need to have a cannon before we need to use a cannon."

And then they'd shift to some drier subject until Granger got distracted by some bug or a flower.

But now Shankon had embarked on one of his lectures, beginning with the sciences and winding up, Granger was sure, in the philosophies. People had told Granger that Shankon had been a great teacher, sought out by pilgrims from beyond the horizon, undaunted by the miles to wisdom.

Shankon always brushed off questions about that history, but one thing was clear to Granger: the old man could spin a tale.

"Gunpowder gives the cannon its muscle," Shankon was saying. He pointed to a rock about half the size of the lad's head. "Lift that stone and throw it as far as you can."

Granger grunted, and watched the little boulder thud down a couple of feet in front of him.

"Now with a cannon and its gunpowder, we could shoot that a furlong and a half with a sound that itself would be as frightful as that hurtling ball of death.

"And the gunpowder? It's nothing but an admixture of sulfur, saltpeter and charcoal. Simple ingredients. Awesome results."

He checked to see that Granger's eyes were suitably wide before he went on.

"And what do you suppose are the ingredients of a dragon's turd?" He cocked the eyebrow again.

"I don't know."

"What?"

"I don't know, *sir?*"

"Well, the science tells us that a dragon's turd consists of sulfur and saltpeter. And if the dragon has lately eaten a charred peasant, that poor bugger supplies your charcoal.

"And to ease its digestion, a dragon swallows rocks—bigger than that one at your feet—to crush and grind the cursed meals in its gullet.

"So when these beasts fill our skies, as now they do," he shook his fist upward, "They rain gunpowder on our fields, along with their worn digestive stones. The poison chokes our crops to starve us down, to weaken our resolve. But mark this: they are sowing the seeds of their own destruction."

Granger grew uncomfortable with Shankon's silence. "What do you mean?" he asked, his voice breaking, when he couldn't stand it anymore.

"The stones can be our cannon shot. The dragon shit our powder. We have everything we need to blast them out of the sky, save the cannons themselves." Shankon threw down his fist as if casting the dice of fate.

"How do we get the cannons?" Granger wondered. Even

at his age, he could see the elegance of this plan.

"Men! Only men can build cannons!" Shankon declared, and his pulse seemed to slow down even as the lad watched. "But men are such fools."

The leathery curtain of beating dragon wings continued through the day, the night, and late into the next day. Granger wondered if these were all new dragons overhead, or if they were circling in an arc so huge it seemed straight to his eye, coming around and around, beating, beating.

He and Shankon were safe enough to escape notice under their ledge in the rock face, but just as he wondered if they would ever be able to come out again, the shrieking flock began to thin out. By the next morning the skies had cleared.

And at dawn they saw the four horsemen picking their way up the switchback to their little haven.

"Shankon?" The lead horseman called out. They wore matching tunics, with emblems that Granger didn't recognize. All four were on magnificent dappled grays, but the horses looked tired, no less than the men themselves.

Granger hadn't seen any strangers for a long time, and he was not glad to see these. But the old man just said, "I am."

"Shankon, we come on behalf—"

"I know, I know," Shankon sighed. "What do you think you want?"

The man seemed to be going through a memorized script in his mind, wondering where he should start. For the first time, he noticed Granger, and he gave the boy the slightest nod, and a tiny smile, or grimace, that might have been taken as commiseration.

"Shankon, the scourge of dragons in the Stone River Valley has only increased in recent times."

"Is that right?" Shankon stole a glance at Granger and winked.

"Sir, our traditional defenses have failed, and we've been

instructed to bring you with us to oversee a fresh dragon eradication campaign."

"With complete authority?"

"With generous authority."

"So with the same restrictions the dragons labor under?"

"Sir, the dragons have no restrictions. That is our problem."

"Exactly. And that is my problem, as well."

The lead horseman looked as if he was tempted to consult his troops, but he refrained.

"Shankon, your wisdom and persuasiveness are known far beyond this humble place. We are confident that if you come with us now, you will reach an amicable agreement for your service."

Shankon arched an eyebrow at Granger, who gave a little shrug.

"And are we to walk beside you?" he asked the lead horseman.

"The horses are sturdy. Each of you can ride with one of my lieutenants."

"Better yet, double up your men, and young Granger and I will each take a horse."

And so they rode, as the sun burned off the dew, teasing out the after-scent of yesterday's dragons.

Chapter 2

The Knowledge of Dragons

Long before Shankon's hair bleached out and began to abandon him, he'd been a man whose curiosity and sense of adventure were matched only by his vigor. He toured all the great capitals, roving among their people, sitting their universities, then, years later, rewriting the curricula for those same institutions.

Botany, and its twin sister, Agriculture, were his first loves. His Theory of Agro-Glyphics held that plants communicated vast stores of knowledge through their physical form.

The way the rings of a felled tree told tales of lush and hard years was the most trivial example. In Shankon's vision, each flake of bark, each twist of limb, each shade of a leaf spelled out the history of the Plant Kingdom. The Theory of Agro-Glyphics laid bare the secrets of when to plant and when to lie fallow. In practice, crop yields multiplied, the people rejoiced, and royalty called Shankon to their courts.

Never mind that self-described Shankonists—the very word wrenched his gut—hired themselves out as "forest-readers" and "crop-interpreters" to swindle peasants and nobles alike out of their income. In fact, roving Shankonists, like a new race of quick-eyed, fork-tongued swindlers, would ply their trade long after Shankon's own life had ended.

Next, Shankon turned his attentions to the twin brothers, Mathematics and Physics. With a series of calibrated lenses, he could bring forth a vision of an object at an impossible distance. He labored for years, laying down tables that correlated the speed, arc and weight of a missile compared to the distance of that target. Once he'd completed this, a schoolboy could pluck the answer from his tables.

"Shankon could fell an eagle from a thousand leagues," is how this accomplishment found its way to the ears of influence around the world. That was not exactly the truth, but he saw no profit in correcting the details in the statement.

So by the time he turned his attention to dragons, Shankon was already celebrated across the known world. Courts major and minor vied for his attendance. In addition to his brilliance and charm, he brought a dry wit that endeared him to the thrones.

In addition, he was not an unhandsome man—and well dressed at that—for whom the ladies of the courts lobbied in subtle ways.

But the dragons! He knew from the start that they were an entirely different line of research.

He knew many creatures lived in cycles of hibernation and vitality. The bear abided by its winter respite, the cicada by a seventeen-year slumber. But according to the crumbling scrolls and ancient tablets he'd seen in his travels, the dragons hewed to a much longer, and more purposeful, time frame.

In the oldest texts, a thousand years would pass between scourges. And indeed, in those days, the dragons were bumbling, earth-bound creatures, hard to reconcile with the deathly, writhing flocks that had lately blotted the sun.

But in each re-borning of the dragon horde, they took on new traits. Knobs appeared on their backs in a certain year, and in their next appearance, the dragons sprouted wings—although it took several more generations before they learned to fly with them.

The fangs grew longer. The breath grew hotter. Eyes turned from green to crimson-rimmed yellow.

Even more horrifying to the young scholar Shankon was that the time between re-bornings seemed to be decreasing with each crop. The oldest limestone tablets indicated a thousand-year respite. Then it was seven hundred years. And when papyrus took up the tale, the interval was a mere four hundred years.

Indeed, Shankon's own grandfather had told of a hundred-year respite. Yet this latest crop of dragons emerged on a scale closer to a decade after that last eradication. And each more deadly, more agile, more—could it be true?—cunning than the last.

And here was Shankon. Once celebrated beyond every horizon, the toast of all the world, riding with a band of fools on gray horses to meet The King who'd had the chance to still the dragons years ago, and let it slip.

He had the best horse, and he could take pleasure in that aspect of the ride. Granger looked pleased, as well. The militia, not so much.

Shankon knew so many things he'd become famous for the sheer volume of his knowledge. Indeed, he'd probably forgotten more than any normal man could know. But one thing he could never forget was that he was old, and that his days were numbered. He realized he could apply his Theory of Agro-Glyphics to himself now—each ache in a bone, each halt in a ligament—wrote the story of his life, and of his destiny.

There was little chance he would make it to the next re-borning of the dragons, so this would be his last attempt to bend the awful arc of their ascent.

Chapter 3

On the Road to the King

Once they'd lit the fire for their first night's camp, Shankon gestured to the leader of the soldiers. "Of course, I'm laboring under a disadvantage," he said.

"A disadvantage?" The force of his question betrayed its truth. "You rode our finest horse! And your ward claimed the second finest!"

"And we're most grateful for those accommodations," Shankon nodded and pulled at his beard. "But did you not have my name and some garbled history in the orders that brought you to me? Yet we have nothing to call you except those obvious descriptions, 'Big Man', 'Short Man', 'Pompous Man' and 'Hot-Head'. A distinct disadvantage, wouldn't you say?"

Big Man pursed his lips and fought against a flush in his cheeks.

"Easily remedied," Shankon said, waving his flat palms before him like a mime who'd found a wall.

"You already know that I am Shankon, a philosopher, traveler and council to kings in the near and far lands. I'm sure your orders laid out my peculiarities in some detail. Whether those details were accurate or not is of little concern, at least for the length of our journey.

"My young associate is Granger, assistant thereof and a drinker of knowledge. Unlike me, he scarcely has a history.

But in the fullness of time, it will be a story of great consequence."

If one can bow only from the neck, that's the measure the man gave. "My sincerest apologies." he said. "My men are Paramus, Karamus and Daramus." Each nodded deeply in turn. "Loyal servants to The King. And I am Lawrence, Special Designate Royale."

"And?" Shankon prompted after a moment.

"And?" Lawrence looked puzzled.

"The horses' names?"

The Special Designate Royale's eyes grew large as any of the horses.

"Are we to call them 'Big Gray', 'Little Gray', 'Spirited Gray', and 'Lazy Gray'?" Shankon asked. "If your mission is to bring me to The King, is not 'Spirited Gray' a more valuable player than Karamus, for instance? Surely such a horse has a name!"

Lawrence shook his head in a tight wobble and, to Granger's eye, he himself looked like a horse about to whinny. "The horses are Moonlight, Goblin, Lightning and Old Salt." He pointed to each one as he called their names and, like the men before them, each nodded in turn.

Granger put his hand over his mouth, but nobody was paying him any mind. The men seemed to have a variety of scripts vying for the stage.

They'd followed the ridge over the valley most of the day, unmolested by dragons and in that remote region, they saw no other humans, and little game. They'd finally set their camp in a place that afforded elevation, a rocky cover and the calming scent of sage on the evening breeze.

"You're a good leader, Lawrence, but you worry too much," Shankon said.

"Sir, one cannot live without the other."

"To the contrary, good man. Worry should be reserved for

possibilities, lest it expend itself before it's needed."

Granger had thought—in not so many words—that Lawrence was a handsome man, but step by step this evening, his refined features seemed to be transforming themselves, ever so slowly into an entirely different face.

"So you would have us make an open camp on the plains, exposed to dragons, highway men and rabid dogs?"

Shankon sat down the way he did, slowly, with old, creaking bones, as he had often explained to Granger, and slapped his hands on his knees.

"A highway man foolish enough to come this far in search of anything of value could be easily turned away. I've heard of rabid dogs, but never seen one. I'm sure Daramus or Paramus could dispatch it with an arrow or a dagger, if it came to that.

"As for the dragons, we'll be at The King's banquet long before they give us pause again."

"Where did the dragons go?" Granger chimed in, clamping down on the last word as he realized in horror that he was barging into an adult conversation.

"To Hell, whence they came," Karamus shouted, pounding a fist on his knee.

"That's so good to know, Karamus," Shankon said. "So, in your view, Heaven will always remain high above us?"

"Of course it will!" Karamus said. "I don't take your meaning, Sir."

Shankon studied each face around the campfire slowly, one at a time. Finally, he said, "Hell must be so much more densely populated than the other pole, being loaded down with all those dragons and sinners. The weight of all the evil in the world is just ballast to keep Heaven aloft, always out of our reach.

"Saints are the rarest thing. The rest of us? We'll be forced to join the cursed dragons and scum down there, and suffer their torments once again."

Karamus, reaching for his dagger, shouted, "Blasphemy! And a blasphemer's fate you'll find."

Lawrence was on his feet, touching Karamus lightly on the wrist, as a skilled horsemen would instruct his mount. "Leave thoughts to the thoughtful, Karamus," he said. "And reserve action according to your oath."

Chapter 4

Up from the Garden

Shankon was the first to understand why no ancient skeletal remains have ever been recovered of a creature like the modern dragon.

In his original research, he learned that the earliest dragons were described as serpents, legless wretches with few teeth to fend off the birds of prey or the rats that shadowed them. Guile alone allowed them to survive, either by lurking under cover of the garden's floor, or by writhing with such comic abandon that the predator was disarmed by the spectacle.

One imagined eagles quaking with laughter, jackals starting in disbelief at the sight of these proto-dragons lashing themselves through the dust like penitents paying down the tariff of their sins.

But over the millennia, *Serpentes dragonus* accumulated both offensive and defensive traits with each succeeding generation. The rubbery gums gave way to calciferous ridges, then surging into teeth until their mouths became cages of yellow sabers, driven by bone-crushing jaws.

The smooth underbelly sprouted stubs that articulated into paws, and in turn into claws that could squeeze a sentry's soul from his helpless body even before a last scream could emerge.

The foul breath in due course ignited, and then extended both its temperature and range.

The wings—they learned to use them soon enough—grew in size until their draft could lay even a large man flat in the mud. Shankon read accounts of a dragon wing's wind embedding a straw in an oak, just as a skilled archer might sacrifice an arrow. But he was never able to verify this particular feat.

And while the dragons made themselves into more perfect killing machines, they also built up their defenses. Their scales grew so thick an arrow had to negotiate the seam between two plates to have any effect. While the tempest of their wings could flatten cities, it could also speed them away from any attack, although men had fewer and fewer means of threat in any case.

So the guile that had preserved them in the infancy of this terrible breed seemed less important as their physical character advanced. But the guile itself never diminished.

And in these latter years, Shankon was convinced, with a certainty that roiled his gut and pumped acid up his throat, that the reptilian intelligence had been evolving apace over all these many years.

Mankind—yes, he had to admit it—had not made similar gains, neither physical, nor mental. If a spell overnight gave dragons speech, the evil beasts could no doubt persuade their victims to march to their doom, cheering themselves along the way as their fellows burst one by one into flame.

The reality was all the more bitter because Shankon knew it didn't need to be this way. He'd been so close the last time. He held little hope that his rendezvous with The King in three days would make a difference. But the journey gave him time to reflect.

The journey—hope played out over the course of a road— was really all one had.

Until even that was taken.

Chapter 5

Where Did the Dragons Go?

As a young student, eager to drink in all the world's knowl-edge, Shankon had disciplined himself to sleep lightly. Any disturbance in the night was a welcome excuse to light the oil and thumb through an ancient text until dear Hypnos emerged to lure him back to the shadows.

But the vice that had once brought such pleasure, had become, in his elder years, an affliction. No breeze was too slight, no shooting star too dim, no opossum too stealthy to fail to rouse him.

So by the time Granger whispered, "Uncle Shankon!" in his ear, his eyes were already full wide.

"I'm not your uncle, lad. What is it at this hour?"

"You're a kind of uncle," Granger whispered. "You said as much yourself."

"As you wish, young man. Did you come to discuss gene-alogy on this moonless night?"

Granger moved closer still to Shankon's ear, lest he be heard by the others. "The dragons!" he said. "If they didn't go to Hell, where did they go?"

Shankon grunted, and with some effort rose up on his elbow.

"Look in the sky," the old man said, and they both craned their necks to take in the spangled ceiling of the night. "Is not the absence of dragons sufficient? Do you need ten leagues of separation to find comfort? A hundred? A thousand?"

Granger turned this over a few times. "Perhaps a thousand."

"And what comfort is that, if the speed of the monsters can outstrip the swiftest hawk? A thousand-league flight might pass in the blink of a serpent's eye."

Granger's feet scrabbled the dirt. "You're scaring me!"

"But what would you do differently right now if their wings once again blotted out the stars?"

A long silence passed that Shankon, not Granger finally interrupted.

"Cower beneath a boxwood bush? Cry out to raise an army from the wilderness? Load your sling? What thing would you do that you're not doing now?"

A river of thoughts swept over Granger, but there was little for him to cling to against the current, save this, "What good is it to grow old then, if there are no answers, even to a boy's questions?"

Shankon couldn't help but laugh, and he resolved to have that overdue conversation about genealogy with young Granger, if they both survived the year.

"My words are not meant to rile you, but to soothe you, dear lad." He lay back on his roll and pulled Granger closer to him. "Each day is a tapestry of gifts and taxes. If you view each day as a ledger, you'll miss the subtle beauty of a life gone by.

"Am I not the oldest person you've ever met?"

Granger nodded in the dark, but when Shankon squeezed him for a response, he whispered, "Yes, sir. You surely are."

"And yet there was a time when men of my age transformed the world. They went out, with full heads of hair, and made laws and saw their inventions take shape, and their arguments hold the day. It's hard for you to believe, and to be true, it strains my own imagination now.

"But so many of my generation eyed that ledger—this day's gift weighed against that day's tax—that they raced to early graves from fear of what that final balance would read. Some were even gone before their hair turned gray. Who among them would have thought that my own sparse, white mane would be the trophy that those movers and shakers of the world all coveted?"

"So you don't know if you've had more good days than bad?" Granger asked, snuggling in under the old man's armpit as a breeze lifted smoke from the fire's embers.

"Goodness, I've got a precise tally!" Shankon snorted. "You keep the score in your heart, not in treasure or fame. And unless I very soon make an error beyond measure, the sum of my life will leave you in the cups."

They both lay quiet for awhile, looking up at the imperceptible procession of stars across the night.

"I don't know if you took my meaning," Shankon said at last.

"I think so." Even as he said it, Granger began to wonder if he did know what Shankon meant.

"The point of it is, that the dragons will come and the dragons will go," Shankon sighed. "When they are here, there is little you can do that you have not prepared for in advance.

"But when they are gone, you have time to lay your plans."

"Oh," Granger said, dragging the syllable out.

"But nowhere in a productive scheme is there room for the paralysis of fear. Recognize your foe. Analyze the problem. Devise the solution."

"Convince your allies," is the part Shankon held back that night.

But he went on, "And to answer your original question, if the dragons remain true to their history, they are making their way to the headwaters of the Stone River, three days' flight from here. Again, if history is any indication, they'll spend a few days feasting on mortals and beasts, primping their wings and belching fire before flocking back this way."

Granger's feet kicked out involuntarily.

"So we'll be in the court of The King by then to see what good we can do there. But history also indicates that whatever the dragons did in the past, they can do with greater speed, ferocity and skill now.

"So our task is urgent," Shankon said, yet couldn't resist adding, "And our escorts are anchors."

Shankon could not see Granger's smile in the starlight, and soon they both drifted back to sleep.

Chapter 6

Passage through a Barren Land

They mounted just past dawn and dipped their heads against the sun for several hours as they rode due east. From time to time, Shankon broke into song, much to the annoyance of Karamus and Daramus, whose discipline allowed no more outlet than a scowl.

A maiden sublime, I once knew,
She had a come-along smile,
It lasted only awhile,
And I looked for a maiden anew.

Shankon possessed that rare singer's voice that repels even its owner, but he found sport in their reaction. Granger screwed up his face and did a mime's work on his ears. At least he was in on the joke.

But if he sang for long, his throat developed an itch and he had to go to the skin for a drink. He knew better than to waste his water.

When they had room to go two abreast, the four militia men, on their two horses, took the lead. When the trail narrowed to single file, Lawrence and Karamus led on their horse, followed by Shankon, Granger, and the Daramus and Paramus team providing rear cover.

The recent hail from the dragons was already doing its work on the landscape. The grass had browned out, the trees seemed ill, and an oily sheen slowed the river's current beneath the morning mist. The bleak surroundings soured the mood of the entire company, as they trod on, hour by hour, day by day.

In spite of Lawrence's beard, Granger could see the set of the man's jaw and read its message of resolve. Granger, young as he was, thought Shankon might best tread lightly here, as with a dog whose leash has not yet been tested.

Such thoughts would never have occurred to Shankon who saw Lawrence tracing back in his mind every ambition, every choice, every whim of fate that had brought him to this particular, wretched place. There were so many noble ways to serve The King. Why had he drawn this straw?

"Captain," Shankon called out to the man ahead. "You must be a man of some substance for The King to entrust you with my safe journey."

A moment passed before Lawrence turned his head slightly to the horse's off side and said, "I'm a servant to The King. I have neither desire nor ability to divine his motives."

Karamus turned and spat off the horse's near side. "We've led swine to market on The King's orders, as well as the likes of you."

"Karamus," Lawrence looked straight ahead as he addressed his man. "Whether swine or saint is your cargo, you have sworn to The King to seal your lips as to the nature of your mission."

Karamus shook his head and deflated. "Aye," he croaked.

They made thirty or thirty-five miles a day at a walk, and they held to that pace due to the stress on the lesser horses that Shankon had engineered by doubling up the soldiers on their backs.

From time to time, when the trail widened, Shankon

would cluck and nod to Granger, and they'd gallop past their escorts, and wait, laughing, around the next bend. The soldiers failed to appreciate this small humor.

"Dear Lawrence," Shankon said that afternoon, bored by the plodding progress. "We know the way to our destination. Why don't the lad and I go on ahead, and you fellows can arrive at your leisure?"

"I cannot allow that, good sir."

"You realize I have known The King since before you were born?" Shankon tilted his head to see if Lawrence would turn back to show any reaction. "In fact I knew his father quite well, and his father's father to a lesser measure, before the royal disease bled them both out.

"The King once sat on my lap and took a schoolboy's pleasure in my stories." Shankon trailed off, then started up again, "So long ago. But nothing has really changed except our ages, or infirmities. I expect he wants me to tell those tales once again, so that he can recapture the comfort, the certainty that only a schoolboy can enjoy."

The conversation's clockwork ran awry as Lawrence searched for both answers for himself, and another set of answers that he might utter out loud.

"The King knows what is best," is what he finally settled on.

"Yet The King employs council to advise him on what's best. And if that fails, he casts a wider net, which, I submit, you are pulling in at this moment, dear Lawrence.

"I cannot see the future, nor can I read a deck, a cast of sticks, or the entrails of a chicken to reveal what may or may not come to pass. But I can predict that the sun will rise tomorrow. And with the same certainty, I can tell you that The King wants his comfort, and perhaps those stories he heard on my knee were the last time he felt such comfort.

"Whether he can see beyond the comfort and take the

council is what will decide my fate. And perhaps yours, my good sir.

"And perhaps the whole world's."

They'd just entered a broad plain and Shankon gave a cluck and a nod to Granger and the two of them spurred their horses past the soldiers.

When they'd reached fifty yards, Lawrence, seeing the game had changed this time with no curve ahead for his tormentors to stop and wait for their pursuers, called out. "Shankon! Where are you going? Wait, on order of The King!"

By the time the racing horses had reached half a furlong's lead, Lawrence shouted to Karamus, "Get off. Get off you fool!"

Karamus: "What?"

Lawrence swung his elbow back, unseating his passenger, and spurred his horse in pursuit. After several miles, he ran down his quarry, and they waited for Karamus, Daramus and Paramus to finally arrive, much later, atop a gray gelding that was done for the day.

Chapter 7

Admission to the Court

While Daramus tended the spits that held the hares that would make supper that evening, Lawrence passed a wine skin around the fire. The company's divisions began to blur. And on the second rotation of the skin, Granger wobbled to his feet, looked around uncertainly, and plopped back down again.

"I myself have never met The King," Lawrence was saying, blotting his lip against his sleeve. "I've heard his voice only from afar on Arvon's Day. And yet I obey his every whim without question. While you, learned sir, claim a close acquaintance, yet you weigh The King's desires on some scale visible to you alone."

Shankon nodded and stroked his beard. "One might form such an impression."

"So pray tell, good man, how did you first gain a seat in the court? What talent or charm or bit of trickery brought you to that table where purple blood is the only currency? Surely you are not a noble yourself?"

Shankon clapped his hands on his knees and laughed. "I assure you, my blood is as red and thin as yours, dear Lawrence. But as to your point, I am who I am, and as ever I have been and shall be. Beyond that, would you have me speculate as to The King's motives? Earlier on this very day, I swear I heard you say that you would do no such thing your-self."

"Bah!" It was Lawrence's turn at the skin, but he held it as he formulated his thoughts. "You are not bound by my code, nor I by yours. We have heard that you are a great teacher. So educate us in how a commoner might find favor at the highest table."

"Such a lesson might sound like boasting—though I take no pride in it—and that would be a bad example to set for young Granger." Shankon nodded at his ward, but was caught off guard to see the boy asleep with his head on a rock.

Lawrence took his turn to burst out laughing. "He'll pay you no mind, so out with your story!"

Shankon shrugged. "So many details are lost over a span of years, and indeed each of the players would see it through his own lens," he said, gathering his thoughts as if they were sheep that had strayed across the range. "But I'll grant you my recollection on the condition that some of the principals might challenge this or that aspect, just as I might challenge their version."

"Lawrence," Daramus called out with a catch in his voice. "The hares are near done."

"Not now, damn it, Daramus. Temper your fires." Turning back to Shankon, he nodded. "Understood. Please proceed."

"Very well." Shankon brought the flats of his hands together, as if in prayer, took a deep breath, and rolled his head around slowly, working out any kinks in his posture. And he began, "From an early age, I set to traveling the world in pursuit of knowledge. I attached myself to a succession of mentors. I believe I had one advantage over the numberless young men taking a similar path."

"And what was that?" Lawrence prompted him, impatient.

"The common approach to apprenticeship in those days, and I'm certain it has not changed, was for the student to perform the most menial tasks the master demanded in exchange for tidbits of knowledge which would—at great length—enable the apprentice to make his way in the world.

"My own approach—and nobody instructed me in this—was to study the master's path to his own mastery. I did all the same vile chores and learned all the techniques and skills that advantaged my fellows. But in each instance, I became the master's favorite student, because I begged for the lessons of his life, even more than the lessons of his craft, or field of study."

Lawrence was about to rise up in exasperation, but Shankon waved him down. "Pass the wine skin, young Lawrence, and I'll answer your objection."

Shankon took his draught and went on, "You feel I tried to deny you the lessons of my own life, even as I admit to advancing myself through the life lessons of my own mentors. True enough, and you are a shrewd student of human nature to recognize that. It's no wonder The King has such high regard for you!"

Lawrence may have blushed, but it was slight enough to be explained away by a flare up from a drop of hare grease in Daramus's cook fire.

So Shankon told how he toured the known world in his early decades, with each stop bringing him new skills, new knowledge, more experience. It was not, he pointed out, unlike the way the dragons marked each new emergence on the time line of history with more deadly powers than before. The difference was that Shankon's developments were for the ultimate benefit of mankind, rather than its destruction.

In any case, young Shankon was seeking a patron so he might advance his theory of Agro-Glyphics, when a noble with holdings in the province where Shankon had becamped took notice of the increased yields at harvest. After a series of interviews, Shankon gained admittance to the Castle of The King.

This was the father of the sovereign now known as The King. And this was on the very eve of the expected return of the dragons. On their last rampage, the monsters had laid to waste great swaths of the kingdom, which were only now beginning to recover.

Thousands of serfs had been incinerated, along with their stock, and—let's call him The Old King to be clear—The Old King sorely missed his taxpayers.

The Old King, who reigned with brilliance and wisdom over every detail of his kingdom, had for years railed against his advisors who time after time failed to stem the destruction of the dragons. It was all so predictable. And the fools were all so useless.

So why not seek counsel from this new arrival, so highly commended for his expertise with crops? Surely brilliance in one field would spill over into another?

The part Shankon omitted from his retelling was that one of his many mentors had taught him that if he didn't know an answer, he should never admit it, but rather beg time to discover it. And that was the advice Shankon employed when The Old King sought his help against the next wave of dragons.

"With your limitless resources and virtue," the young Shankon declared without blinking, "we shall surely prevail. If it pleases you, I will formalize a plan."

This was the best news The Old King had received on the subject in quite some time. Most often, he was met with hand-wringing and ducked heads from his meal-brained court.

The kingdom, yea the world, had never seen a plan such as Shankon devised.

He proposed filling sheeps' bladders with a caustic substance—fine lye would do nicely—and wrapping the bladders in fish nets. The nets would be attached to parasols donated by ladies of the court—pink or green, yellow or blue—held closed by the lightest thread.

When the dreaded dragons flocked, the catapults would let fly and when each parcel reached its peak, the parasol would open to ease the descent of the lye-bladder. And as this contraption floated into the midst of the beasts, the long bows would take aim, burst the bladders and release clouds of lye that would blind the spawn of Hell and leave them powerless.

"Does he take us for fools?" Simpson, The Old King's most trusted confidant shouted, on hearing of the scheme. "Our only prayer would be that the dragons would die laughing."

"And what better idea have you?" The Old King scowled. And what success have you had as with each emergence the dragons have wrought greater havoc?"

"My Lord, it's preposterous on the face of it. No good can come from this!"

The Old King looked at his old friend coldly. "If the world has gone mad, then it's madder still to follow the old madness. We will follow this new madness. Let it be written.

"Let it be known."

And so the orders went down and the butchers and larders and parasol factors ramped up their efforts. New catapults were lashed together. The bowmen practiced their art.

The low people loved it. They had no idea what place their crafts took in the plan, but they enjoyed the commerce and sang for unity.

The nobles, by contrast, muttered in the castle's hallways. While they hoped The Old King would succeed in this ridiculous project, they'd been castrated, and they longed to see this upstart join their ranks.

Even when all the preparations had been made, and the

cogs were in place, the weeks slipped by without a sign of the dragons.

For months, the crier's message had been "This may be the day of the dragons. Make your preparations!"

But now he rang his bell and shouted, "The dragons are not done with us."

In any case, he was ignored.

But then the skies darkened again and filled with the deafening shriek and refrain of the monsters. Shankon had schooled an army to execute the plan and he called from the ramparts to rally them to action.

"Catapults, volley!" he shouted through a horn. "Reload!"

The lye bombs flew, floated, and then burst with the arrows as the dragons disappeared in white clouds of poison. The blinded monsters flamed each other in confusion. They tried to rub their eyes with their wings, skewing their flight until they thudded to earth, crippled, where lance horsemen charged past, plucking their gizzards out on the run.

The spectacle outshone even the Arvon's Day celebrations and when it was all over, the kingdom celebrated. Peasants even tried butchering the fallen dragons, but soon found the meat was foul.

Bugles sounded across the miles. Shankon had sealed his place in the court of The Old King.

When he had finished with his tale, his eye surveyed his company. Lawrence, Paramus and Daramus stared into the fire as if its crackle and spark held an important message. Granger snored as lightly as only a child can. But Karamus broke the silence.

"I don't believe a word of it," he hissed at last. "Have you ever heard such nonsense?"

"I sought our guest's history in good faith," Lawrence said, scowling at his man. "And that is how it shall be received." He paused before adding, "Along with the caveats he outlined at the start."

"My good man, are Granger and I considered your guests then? We thought our role aligned more closely with that of a prisoner."

"You wound me, Shankon, just as you have been wounded yourself." Lawrence spread his arms in supplication. "You've told us how you landed in high places. Now, pray, tell us the tale of how you fell from those heights."

Shankon considered this briefly. But he said, "That is a story more fantastic than the last, for it deals not with evil on the wing, but with the follies that drive men's hearts. I'm afraid it would strain this audience." He nodded ever so slightly at Karamus.

"And even so, the hour is late, and young Granger needs a better pillow than that stone, or he'll awaken with a crooked neck."

Chapter 8

The King with No Name

Lawrence came to trust his guests—or captives or cargo, however they cared to style themselves—well enough that they could dash ahead, even out of sight, and he remained calm, assured that his band would eventually catch up with them.

And so, as Granger convalesced under the effects of the night's grog, they broke ahead of the group and Shankon told stories of dragons and war to distract him from his misery while they awaited the soldiers.

"Do you know the story of Arvon? The true story, not the rubbish told on his holiday?" Shankon's eyes seemed to Granger to be asking their own questions that had nothing to do with either Arvon or holidays.

"I don't remember either story," Granger admitted. "I love Arvon's Day for the cannons." He added after a moment, "And the food and the girls."

"The fault is not yours. The story the pot-bellied politicians bleat from the balconies is too self-serving and tedious to register with anyone of your intelligence. And the other, true version, is never heard beyond a whisper."

"What did he do, Uncle?"

Shankon pulled up his horse. "Once again, I remind you I am not your uncle. Not according to any conventional pedigree," he said. "But I see we'll need to address that issue once and for all."

The wind blew out of Granger, so Shankon added, "At a later date."

Granger's headache gradually faded with the soothing rhythms of their horses' steps, and of Shankon's yarn.

"Arvon served as Prime Exemplar in the court of both The Old King, and The Old King's father," Shankon was saying. "But unlike the many lurkers who filled the seats of the court, he lived by his title. He remained loyal to his kings, but just as loyal to truth.

"That allowed him to contradict his sovereign if the facts so demanded. As you grow older, I'm sure you'll appreciate how extraordinary such a position is. Most of the court would sell the truth for tuppence, then try to buy royal favor with the profit."

Shankon spit, not once, but twice, and shook his head mournfully.

"Did you know Arvon, Uh—-?" Granger stopped himself in time.

"No, but The Old King and his father knew him quite well, of course, and they conveyed the details to me."

"Why did they tell you?" Granger's eyes could not have been larger.

"Why indeed?" Shankon seemed never to have considered this before. "Perhaps they thought only fresh ears would learn from such a cautionary tale."

"Well, what did they tell you?"

Shankon tipped a handful of roasted pumpkin seeds from his bag and passed them to Granger. These were the things, Granger would realize many years later, that gave memories their persistence. The texture and flavor, even the subtle, earthy aroma of the seeds bound the story of Arvon to his soul.

And in Shankon's retelling, Arvon's story was rooted long before the great man himself was born. In the earliest history of the kingdom, indeed in its pre-history, the hierarchies of society were much more fluid than they have become. This held some advantages, but its shortcomings were exposed when a marauding army threatened the social order.

The consensus was that all able men should come together to mount a defense, and they quickly sorted out a command structure for each village and its environs.

But one able-tongued man suffered a rare disease that caused him to bleed profusely from the slightest wound. He'd once bled three days and turned white as a ghost from a mere splinter in his finger before the finest physician of the day could staunch the wound.

"I would be such a poor soldier," the wretch admitted, "But my infirmity has given me insight and an analytical mind. It has taught me how to navigate a hostile world. I could best serve our cause by guiding the campaign from a central location. Bring me your intelligence, and I'll bring us victory," he declared.

"In the end, the marauders were repelled and the people were only too glad to proclaim the engineer of the victory as their king," Shankon explained. "Call him 'The Oldest King.' He was the ancestor of The King we are due to meet at the end of this journey, and of The Old King, and of all their antecedents."

Shankon looked at the cool, cloudless sky and drew in a great breath of air.

"The dragon odor has cleared at last," he said, exhaling with a long, satisfied sigh.

They rode along another furlong before Shankon said, "In your studies, you've probably noticed that other great nations give their royals names and numbers. They have their King Thomas III and Queen Beverly VI, and on and on."

Granger nodded enthusiastically. "I know!" He thought he was the only one who had noticed that practice, so different from their own kingdom.

"And we have The King, whoever he happens to be at the time." Shankon couldn't help but smile. "I once knew an old farmer who always had one mule to work his field. He'd been through dozens of animals over the years, but every one he called 'Samuel.' I said, 'Good man, surely each beast has its own qualities, even its own personality. Do they not deserve their own names?'

"And his answer was that despite their qualities and personalities, he needed the same talents from each one of them. And besides, it would drive him mad to keep all the names straight, especially in the fullness of his years as he was when I consulted him on this matter. It was easier for the beast to learn its defaulted name, than for the farmer to separate them in his mind."

Granger looked a little dubious. He had a young mind's knack for soaking up new information, like the names of a dozen mules. Yet, he'd seen enough of the fogginess age brings—not in Shankon, certainly, but in other geezers of his acquaintance—to find this story plausible.

But Shankon brought the story full circle.

"Like that old farmer, the kingdom chose to pare down the royal nomenclature to its simplest terms. The people needed the same rituals from each king, just as that farmer relied on some Platonic ideal of a mule that ever plowed his fields.

"It was that disease of the blood that forced the issue," Shankon snapped his fingers and stared at them in wonder, as if the sound came with a golden aura and the scent of crushed white grapes. He brought the fingers to his nose to savor that aroma, and then went on.

"Just as those over-large ears and the sloping brow that

haunt the walls of the castle's galleries were passed down from generation to generation, so was the infirmity.

"The brasher The King, the earlier his demise, as some fit of temper would break the skin, and set the clock running to the royal funeral. Once The King suffered a sneezing fit when introduced to the palace cats, burst a vessel in his nose, and succumbed three days later. Indeed, coronations became annual affairs for long stretches of the kingdom's history. Peasants would be taken aback by strangers wearing the crown, but their concern never lasted long.

"The royal mint was stretched to the limit, striking new coins and destroying the old at a pace the world has never known. The artists who engraved the master stamps did not suffer so much, because each face bore a strong resemblance to the previous ones. But the coin presses were sorely taxed.

"So who could blame the people for not knowing the name of their leader?" Shankon wondered. "Long live The King!"

Chapter 9

Arvon's Day

They made camp near a spring untouched by the dragons' dander. Despite his faults, Karamus proved himself an arch bowman, and quickly supplied several hare for the supper. Paramus gathered water and tinder, while Daramus foraged for herbs. He wafted a crush of tarragon under all their noses, proud of his find. He secured prime sage, a spray of wild onions, and some root even Shankon could not name that added the perfect, biting accent to the stew.

Lawrence judged there was enough wine left for three or four passes, but Granger begged off this time.

"Would such a feast be complete without a song?" Shankon asked. To him it was a rhetorical question, but it brought concrete answers from the company.

"I'd sooner butcher that fine horse you've stolen and leave you to wander barefoot in the brambles tomorrow than endure such a fate tonight," Daramus was first to declare.

"Aye!" Paramus shouted, and the others quickly concurred.

Rather than looking admonished, Shankon beamed. "Good men! If I'd been able to form a consensus so easily when I was half this age, I might never have left the castle.

"But then there would have been no need for you to fetch me from the hinterlands and we never would have met. So, it seems that all good lessons come in their proper time."

"Except those that come a little too late for the student," Lawrence said, but his expression did not reflect the pessimism of his words. "So give us a tale instead of a song, and we'll judge whether it hits its mark. Your quiver never seems to empty."

Granger saw Shankon run his index finger down the left side of his beard, as if trying to tease a story out of his fine, white hair. But Granger knew by now that Shankon knew exactly which words he would speak. He had a huge catalog of stories, and—as he often said—he'd lived so long he always had a fresh audience.

One time Shankon had told Granger that he wondered if his words held some terrible power, because anyone who had twice-heard one of his stories was dead now. Shankon tried to describe this sad state of affairs solemnly, but even as a kid, Granger saw through the joke.

And so, when Shankon finally clapped his hands on his knees, his voice rang out solid and true through the fragrant shelter pines that ringed their campsite. "Then you shall hear the story of the great hero, Arvon, who preserved the kingdom when even The King thought it lost."

All the men nodded and murmured and Lawrence tapped his forehead for the tale to proceed.

Arvon, in Shankon's telling, had risen through the ranks in the time-worn way, by defending the kingdom in battle. Three strains of men guided the nation's affairs. First and foremost, were the bluebloods of royal lineage—although far from the castle, rakes and cads applied the term 'thin-bloods' with a sneer and a nod to their disease.

Arvon and his ilk were red-blooded warriors, whose courage and leadership demanded a place at the table, even if they were to be ignored by that other class, the nobles, whose blood was purple as a September eggplant, and whose spines swayed easily as wheat in the summer breeze.

In the annual Arvon's Day plays that re-told his story across the kingdom each year, he won the ear of The King—this would be the Father of The Old King—with his brilliant plan to beat back the dragons. Arvon mobilized the kingdom and with pure hearts and plenty of pluck the citizens high and low rallied and sent the evil beasts to their doom.

Around the campfire, the men nodded in recognition. Shankon's summary was familiar to every student. Indeed, every student had first trod the boards in a local production of 'The Saga of Arvon and the Dragons,' regardless of any thespian aptitude or the lack of it.

Shankon stood with his back to the fire, as if warming his hands behind him, although the night was fair.

"But the true story was something else again," he said, spinning and dashing a handful of powder into the flame. The powder flared and gave up green, blue and pure white sparks, along with a cloud of acrid yellow smoke that stung their noses as it rose above the shelter pines.

It was a ridiculous effect, but it won them over, most of all Granger, who appreciated it even more than the rest.

"I'm a shameless old man," Shankon had often confided in the boy. "Nevertheless, if you're ever caught between showing off and pressing a strong case to win the day, favor the spectacle. It closes every argument."

So tonight, Shankon went on with the story behind Arvon's story.

"Arvon did indeed claim a great victory, but his enemy was a more feeble strain than we have come to know," Shankon pointed out. "In those days, dragons were just discovering their powers of fire. Hatchlings were more likely to incinerate their fellows in the den than to threaten any human."

He lurched around the campfire, miming erratic bursts of flame, an artless monster.

"Give Arvon his due!" Shankon stood to his full height and challenged the treetops to contradict him. "His campaign slew every dragon from here to the headwaters. No wonder the people cheered! Never had they known such salvation!

"But he neglected one thing, and like Achilles' heel, it would be his undoing."

Granger waved his arm overhead frantically.

"Yes, master? You have something to add?" Shankon arched an eyebrow.

"The eggs! It was the dragons' eggs that he left!"

"Woe to Arvon, to have not enjoyed young Granger's advice!" Shankon shook his head sadly.

"But perhaps he would have taken that next crucial step, if he'd won over the hearts of the court. Instead, he appealed to The King, who was the underwriter of the entire operation. But the other advisors clawed their way over one other to claim a bit of credit, some tawdry scrap of glory. All the while, they schemed against Arvon himself, eager to see the last of him.

"So when Arvon brought up the matter of the eggs, the coffers of public support were bare. The King himself, The Father of the Old King, found that for the first time in his reign, the people actually recognized him. He was more than a face that flickered across their coins for a season or two. He had achieved currency himself!"

Shankon surveyed the audience, judged that his pun had failed, and brought his arms down.

He pressed on, "The King was the most popular sovereign the kingdom had ever known. Why tax the people any more on a mission whose fruits lay years hence? And with his awareness of his family curse, he knew that the piper would not be paid until long after he was gone. And besides, if Arvon's adventures had been as successful as they seemed, who even knew if far-flung dragon eggs, lying dormant for years, would even be viable without a mothering beast? Perhaps, The King thought, this time would be different."

And so, the dragons suffered a lost generation, but their spawn would avenge them in the fullness of time.

"When Arvon realized he could not muster support to smash those eggs in their foul nests, he did the next best thing," Shankon explained. "He lobbied the court and the people alike to begin girding for the inevitable return of the flock.

"The most learned astrologers had identified a certain alignment in the heavens that seemed to foretell the dragons' return down through the ages. But this cursed cycle of the stars resembled less the movements of clockwork than a boulder racing ever faster down the mountain side."

Lawrence sent the wine skin on its final round. Karamus belched and took a long measure before passing it on to Shankon.

"Tonight we toast Arvon," the old man said, "as with all the martyred saints."

"To Arvon!" the company cried, and Granger jumped up and waved his arms like windmills. "And all the martyrs!"

Shankon took just a spare sip and handed the skin to Daramus.

"In the judgment of those old scholars, even with the acceleration of the dragon's dormant periods, their threat was yet a generation away. Arvon held fast to his mission to re-build the kingdom's capacity to defeat the dragons on their next appearance. But to most people, it seemed so far off that it became a lonely vocation."

Shankon stirred the coals with a stick, searching for some message in their glow.

"Gravity, history, and the folly of man, these are the three immutable laws of nature," he declared at length. "Gravity brings even the eagle back to ground. History repeats itself in an endless cycle, for none take the meaning of its message. And the folly of man? No further words need be spoken.

"Mark these three laws, make your peace with their product, and you can sleep with an untroubled soul."

"But come man, the hour is late," Lawrence piped up. "What fate befell Arvon, if not the glory we were told of in school?"

"The hour is indeed late," Shankon nodded. "As it was for Arvon in his day. Just as he had done before, he engineered an awesome resistance once the threat of the dragons was apparent.

"But in this birthing, they'd enhanced the range of their flames, and mastered their aim as well. As Arvon stood with his troops on the ramparts of the city, he drew his bow against one of the swooping demons and its hot blast crisped him to the bone even as the monster crashed to earth and bled out from the arrow.

"The surviving troops cried his name and renewed their strength. Once again, Arvon had vanquished the dragons, though he could not revel in victory.

"And once again, the battle was won, but the war abandoned, as the next generation's eggs ripened in their lairs.

"And even today, forces cannot be marshaled before it is too late. And so you are here, transporting an old fool to the throne in hopes of salvation. Pray that your efforts are not in vain."

Chapter 10

The Final Leg of the Journey

With full bellies, thanks to the art of Daramus, they all slept soundly that night. Lawrence and his men took comfort in knowing that their commission would soon be discharged. Shankon dozed with the untroubled conscience of one whose counsel could not be corrupted. And Granger dreamt of a great, bustling city, a vibrant place of cannons, pork that melted from skewers into your mouth, and girls with secrets that teased his imagination.

"Ah, but you have seen those walls," Shankon told Granger as they readied their mounts at sunrise. In the slanting light and chill air, the breath of the grays issued from them like ghosts given birth. Song birds began their call and response, along with the notes of some other, coarser birds of the morning.

"What sort of blasted bird is that?" Karamus wondered. "I woke and thought Shankon had broken his oath not to sing!"

"These lands are enchanted, Karamus," Shankon said. "The woods hold the songs they've heard, just as the scrolls held the stories of the past. Each of them, the songs and the stories, sleeps, until their time is ordained."

"Bah!" Karamus grunted and Shankon nodded, smiling through his wispy white beard.

Shankon and Granger cinched their horses and Shankon paused a moment, as if in deep meditation, before heaving himself into the saddle. He noticed that Granger was looking at him strangely.

"Appreciate the simple things, lad," he said. "While they are still simple."

They set off, knowing the others would catch up soon enough and scold them and curse their ancestors. With two dozen miles to go through the foothills, they would easily reach the gates well before nightfall.

"Why do you say I've seen the city?" Granger asked after awhile. "How could I have seen that and forgotten it?"

Shankon watched a hawk swoop down from a great height, skimming the field and rising up again with a serpent lashing from its beak.

"And our thanks to you, noble bird," he said, before turning back to Granger. "There's a river we cross somewhere between birth and childhood, just as there is a river to cross at the other end of our journey.

"You're closer to the one river, and I to the other, young man." Karamus studied his protégé's face. "In each case, the ferryman's toll is all that we brought to the bank of that river.

"At that first river, you surrender the memory of the gasping terror of your birth, when you cried out with ferocity that outstripped your size. You gave up the details of so many painful lessons—the abrasions of learning to crawl, the bruises that came with your first steps, the frustration of finding that art of tongue that would make the world understand you.

"Those are the tolls demanded by the first river crossing.

"But for that second crossing, the price is much steeper, because we accumulate so much more in that leg of our journey. Some of those coins, no doubt, we are glad to be rid of. But we give up the gold along with the copper.

"As people of a certain age, we reckon that the first toll brought good value because our lives are so much more subtle and richer than those we knew as infants. The popular notion, therefore, is that second crossing will be a profitable trade as well. The contrary view of the ledger is too discouraging for most of mankind to consider. Again, that's why the first notion is popular."

Granger's face looked stricken, as Shankon quickly recognized.

"How old are you again, young man?"

"I guess I can't tell you because I don't remember when my aging began," Granger snapped.

This reminded Shankon of himself at such an age. And it also reminded him that there were certain genealogical complexities that he would soon need to reveal to his ward.

"Forgive me if I strayed from my course," Shankon said, bowing as deeply as he could in the saddle. "I meant to explain why you don't remember the city of your birth. And the reason is simply because that tender memory was one of the coins you proffered to cross that first river I spoke of.

"I dare say the faces of your mother and father also contributed to that bounty. A steep price. But without it, you would not be here today."

Shankon saw Granger's expression soften, so he pressed his luck and added, "Enjoying my company."

"Sheesh!" Granger said, just as they heard the soldiers catching up with them.

"Good sir," Lawrence called out. "I must ask you to be less playful and more keen to our goals today."

"Lest you be embarrassed at the gates?"

"If that is how you wish to interpret my request, and if it results in your compliance, so be it." Lawrence shook his head, counting hours in his mind.

Again, Shankon smiled and nodded. He surprised himself by enjoying this passage, and the anticipation of its outcome.

As they drew closer to the city, and to the castle of The King above it, they began to see peasants trailing ox carts in the fields, loading them with the digestive stones and the fecal gunpowder the lately swarming dragons had left behind.

Shankon put little stock in omens, but this at least showed that some person of influence had the sense to review the notes and records he'd preserved before his untimely departure all those years ago.

If not hope, he felt a sort of meta-hope. That is, he could at least hope that there was hope for a better outcome this time.

Now and again they would meet a rider or two going out on some provincial business. All would exchange greetings, a few bits of news and assessments of the weather before the travelers would follow their points on the compass.

With the sun high, the band paused to eat a little goat cheese and unleavened bread while they watered the horses. Daramus spied some grapes which made the perfect complement.

"You'll miss me now, won't you, old man?" Karamus asked as they leaned back against their pines.

"I confess I am not the archer I once was, sir," Shankon said. "So no doubt I will miss you, good man."

And even Karamus had to laugh.

They rode perhaps another hour when a man—not a peasant by his dress, but a city man—rode towards them at high speed, his eyes wild as he grew near enough to make them out. The man waved his arms and shouted something beyond language as he bolted past.

Only Granger had the presence to heel his horse and sprint after the maniac. He trotted back a few minutes later, both Granger and his horse panting, as the mad rider threw up dust in the distance.

"A dragon," Granger gasped. "He said a dragon circled the city."

At once, the party's faces grew gray as their horses.

According to history—according to Shankon—the dragons should be days away from returning.

"How can that be?" Lawrence wondered, on behalf of his men—and on behalf of Granger, for that matter.

"Dear Lawrence, do you recall that I told you that you worry too much?" Shankon asked.

"I do."

"And that worry should be reserved for those times it is truly necessary, lest it be spent too soon?"

"That too, I recall."

"Well, Lawrence," Shankon passed his hand over his face, as if trying to dress it with a better expression, "Now you may worry."

Chapter 11

Passage through the City

At their first glimpse of the city, still several miles distant, Granger looked to Shankon to confirm that such a wondrous sight could be true. But the old man seemed unmoved.

"Hmm? What's that you say?"

"Why didn't you tell me it would be like this?"

Shankon looked bewildered by the question. "I told you from the start it would be a long ride. Don't you remember? But patience. We're nearly there."

When they finally reached the gates in the mighty wall, Lawrence bade Karamus dismount, and then he broke ranks to announce the password to the sentry. The guard eyed the motley band behind Lawrence, scowled and signaled the doorsmen to spread the gate.

Inside the walls, four burly men heaved the ratchets that granted entrance, a few tortured inches at a time.

Shankon had not thought about it much before, but now he marveled at the sheer inefficiency of this mechanism. If troops, or crowds of citizens in flight were desperate to go either in or out of the city, their fate fell to the mercy of these brutes at their levers. Never mind that well placed artillery could breach the wall for any invading hordes.

At length, the sentry declared, "You may pass."

They would traverse the city's broad main avenue, exit

the far gate, and continue through the foothills to the castle, saving an hour over circling the perimeter.

Granger thought it unfair that they couldn't stop at the market stands where ducks in rough cages sold alongside swaths of the finest silks. Cumin, now lilacs, now sweet roasting pork captured his nose, and every color of the rainbow caught his eye.

"Can't we stop for just a moment?"

"We'll have time enough for that later," Shankon said. "But only if we make our haste now."

With his inexperienced eye, Granger failed to notice the frenzied activity just beyond the market street. Up and down the neighborhoods, citizens were toting sturdy planks and sand bags, stocking quivers, filling every jug with water. Preparing for siege.

"Study it well, Granger," he said. "For it may be some time before we see such a sight again."

At length, they came to the far wall of the city, waited impatiently for the doorsmen to do their work, and then proceeded four abreast on the broad road up to The King's castle. Even the horses sensed that their journey was nearly done, and their steps became more lively, their noses keen to the wind.

They rounded the last bend, and instead of the surly challenge of a gatesman, they were met with a herald of sixteen trumpets, their red and gold banners swaying. When the final note faded, a man no taller than Granger, but with the face of a journeyman, bedecked in finery and standing formal as a bishop, unreeled a scroll and read in a voice that belied his size.

"Let it be known that worthy Shankon shall enjoy all hospitalities of the castle. The servants of the Royal Household shall do his bidding. No request shall be questioned and none considered too trifling to fulfill. May he report any dissatisfaction directly to The King on penalty of death to those found at fault. By order of The King!"

The trumpets gave another tattoo as the little man bowed and swept his arm towards the drawbridge. "I expect Sir Lawrence knows the way," he said.

"As do I," Shankon said. "Thank you good sir! And the highest compliments to your brass! Their notes sounded from heaven itself."

Across the drawbridge, they dismounted and gave their horses over to smartly dressed grooms who led them to a reward of water, oats, and rest.

The doors of the The King's home opened as they approached, as if by magic.

Lawrence nodded to Shankon and said, "It has been an interesting journey, sir. I would hope we can share our memories at a later date."

Both of Shankon's eyebrows rose, like albino caterpillars fleeing north. "Lawrence, good Lawrence! Neither flattery nor lying becomes you. Won't you join us in our audience? I wager it will provide a store of tales to dole out to your grandchildren one day."

Lawrence gave a wry grin and rolled eyes that his men could not see. "You are too kind, but I have never met The King myself, and this would be an awkward time. In any case, I have instructions to the contrary."

"Never met The King?" Shankon glanced at Granger as if for confirmation that such a thing was possible. "Then I will doubly miss your company, for that would be an encounter for the ages."

"Good day, Shankon."

"And good day to you, Lawrence. And to you, Karamus. And Daramus and Paramus. May your next mission be less arduous!"

The men nodded and turned to leave. Shankon clapped a

hand on Granger's shoulder. "And so, we shall meet The King!"

Chapter 12

The Late Visitor

The debates never ended as to the origins of dragons. Whence this chimera with the body of a snake, the head of a lizard, a scorpion's bite, the claws of a bear and the mercy of a spider? How could a mortal beast spit flame? How could one creature offer so many paths to death?

The naturists held that, like any species, the dragons were fulfilling their own destiny, just as man has done, by developing new traits through the generations, the better to rule their world.

The philosophers argued that mankind was the crown of creation, and the mere existence of such a paragon of a species demanded the existence of a breed as base as the dragon, so that their evil could lend a balance to the universe.

The mystics laid the blame on some drunken sorcerer—his name lost to antiquity—whose curse unleashed this calamity. His stupor was presumed because what else could account for such a bungled spell as this? In this portrayal, the magician himself was the dragons' first victim.

While the merits of these theories were weighed, common people died by the hundreds with each return of the dragon. They would have much preferred weapons and defenses over the authenticated pedigree of damnation.

And yet this discussion is precisely what the Archbishop had brought to Shankon's step many years earlier, just as Shankon was mapping out strategies and contingencies in his last great war on the dragons.

In hindsight, Shankon knew he should never have cracked the door that night. But he did.

"Your Grace, I'm surprised to see you at such an hour," he said, wary that his visitor might be on a fund-raising mission.

"May I come in?" The Archbishop was a large man, clad in velvet and furs and bearing a face that could have passed without notice in the great gallery of royal portraits. He had a way of asking questions that were not questions. Just as he had a way of giving answers that were not answers. "It's most important."

Shankon glanced over his shoulder, trying to assess his quarters with a stranger's eye. So he was not surprised by the Archbishop's frown as the big man looked slowly from corner to corner as he ducked through the doorway.

"You've been here some time, haven't you Shankon?"

"Yes, Your Grace. Let's have a seat at the table." Shankon gestured, then realized that the table was covered with the maps, measures and plumb strings he'd been using to plot his campaign. He swept the material up and carried it into the adjacent room where he placed his tools on the bed.

"Would you care for a glass of wine? A touch of brandy?"

The Archbishop sighed. "I rarely drink brandy," he said. "But this may be such a time. Fetch the bottle, if it pleases you."

Shankon laid the table, and the Archbishop got to the point.

"The King has entrusted you to defend the kingdom against the imminent peril. He has confidence in your ability to do so, and far be it from me to question The King's judgment.

"But for a man in your position, I expect a comprehensive knowledge of the theories of dragons would be the cornerstone for any action. Don't you agree?"

Shankon, who had more, and darker, hair in those days, scratched his head. He was, frankly, tired. "I'm not sure I take your meaning," he said.

"Let me explain," the Archbishop replied, refilling his snifter. "There are three conflicting narratives about how dragons have become the threat they are today."

As the candlelight flickered in his guest's eyes, Shankon recognized that the Archbishop had begun fueling his passion, either with wine or brandy, during his earlier rounds this evening.

"Certainly, there are even more conjectures out there, but only these three have taken hold in the public forum. And they are the naturist, the philosophical, and the mystical views of the origins of the modern dragon."

Of course Shankon had mastered these concepts early in his charge, but at the time of this meeting, he still abided by political manners and decorum. He granted some rein.

And soon regretted it. The Archbishop droned on about the intricacies of each of these theories, refreshing his snifter at an alarming rate.

The clockwork in Shankon's head ticked down to the hour when he would need to arise and deliver his plan to The King. The candles burned down. Shankon wondered idly if, when they flickered out in little wisps of smoke, the Archbishop would realize it was time to reach his conclusion.

But the big man's discourse had gradually deteriorated so that now he seemed to be seducing the bottle of brandy in hushed tones, oblivious to Shankon.

"I shall be retiring now," Shankon said. "You are welcome to carry on, but if you leave, please take care to shut the door against vermin."

Shankon moved his maps and kit to the floor and dropped instantly into a heavy sleep.

Just prior to his awakening, he dreamt of a strain of dragons that had developed the power of speech. In the nature of dreams, this breed sent an emissary to Shankon to negotiate a truce.

They met in the courtyard and Shankon remarked on the novelty of a dragon that could communicate.

"Your words are not that difficult for us," the dragon replied. "But we do have idioms that are troublesome for you."

And as the dragon widened its mouth, Shankon recoiled at the first jet of fire that jolted him out of his dream.

Chapter 13

Who Would Have Left Such a Place?

An attendant led Shankon and Granger to their apartment, pointed out its amenities and related their schedule.

Their quarters were an improvement on what Shankon had known in the past, and for Granger, they were luxury beyond imagination. He marveled at the tapestry that dominated one wall. He caressed the perfect, polished surface of the table, and hefted each statue on the mantel, as if judging its weight. He plunged his nose into the spray of flowers and drank in their sweet scent.

"Shankon?" he asked once he'd made a complete circuit of the main room.

"Yes?"

"Why in the world did you leave the kingdom before?" For the first time in his life, he gave Shankon the kind of look one might give a crazy uncle.

Shankon took a seat at the table, but Granger did not join him just yet. "Let's say they didn't want me," he said. "And I certainly didn't want them."

Granger rested both hands on the other end of the table and leaned forward, rocking a little on his heels. "Were they bad people?"

Shankon sank into an expression Granger had seen a few times before. The old man's eyes narrowed, he pursed his lips and seemed to breathe more deeply. He'd once described it to

Granger as a host of competing thoughts doing battle, like gladiators, inside his head. And all he could do was wait until one triumphed.

"No, they weren't bad people," he said at last. "At least most of them were not.

"But understand that our mission pitted us against the dragons. In that arena, even the most spineless, despicable greed-hound ranked with greater honor than even the most noble of the dragons—if you can even countenance nobility in hell-spawned lizards such as those."

"But if they weren't bad, why did you leave?"

Shankon withdrew for a moment while his little thought gladiators drew their weapons once again. But this one was a brief interlude.

"Purity is not a characteristic of mankind, young Granger. That concept will become increasingly clear over the course of your long, and celebrated life. But for now, you may accept it simply for the sake of discourse.

"You see, none of us are perfectly good, although that is the flattery we tell ourselves. Nor are any of us perfectly bad. Even the most miserable, back-stabbing, bureaucratic wretch on The King's court has some redeeming quality, though it may take a powerful lens to find it.

"In many cases, it wasn't a case of 'badness' so much as meekness, and sometimes that is worse than being bad. For a bad foe can be vanquished, but a meek ally is a weed that may endure forever.

"In any case, let's say the scales that weighed the collective good against the collective bad had tilted out of balance."

Granger still looked dubious.

"To an alarming degree," Shankon added.

Just then the meal servers announced themselves from the hallway. "We bring roast duck, potatoes, carrots, grapes and a cask of wine," they said, as if this were ordinary fare.

And for awhile, Granger forgot his questions as he engaged with the warmth and the juice of the duck's flesh.

Shankon smiled as he watched Granger feast, and when the boy came up for air, he asked, "A touch of wine, perhaps?"

"No, thank you, sir," Granger said, pushing his chair back from the table a little way.

The boy was a quick study, Shankon thought.

They sat on plush cushions before the fire and Shankon brought up their schedule.

"Tomorrow, when we meet The King, I expect he'll be on his throne, which is some distance from the door," Shankon said. "There is a long, narrow carpet that leads from the door to the base of the throne. It's customary for visitors to stop near the end of this carpet, and kneel with the right knee elevated and head bowed until released by The King. We'll know the spot by the wear left by the knees of the supplicants before us."

Granger nodded through these instructions. "I understand."

"Just follow my lead and everything will be fine," Shankon said.

"Yes, sir."

"But there is one other point."

"Yes?"

"At my stage of life, the body's gristle becomes like bone, and the bone becomes like gristle, and unpracticed movements are fraught with stiffness and pain. Do you take my meaning?"

"I'm not sure that I do, sir."

"When the time comes for us to kneel before The King, I may need to lean on you a bit for balance to assume the posture. He won't mind, and my hope is that you won't either."

Granger recognized this as a pivotal moment. The man who had been his de facto father, the only father he had ever known, his protector and tutor, would now rely on Granger's strength and resilience, even if only in this one, simple task.

"Very well," he said, without missing a beat.

"Perhaps we should rehearse the motions now?" Granger said, looking into the fire. "Just to make sure the performance will be flawless?"

And so they practiced the routine three times, walking from the door to the fireplace, and taking a knee. Indeed, on the first trial, Shankon's descent was both lengthy and awkward. But by the third time, as his sinew loosened, he could find his position reasonably well with Granger's support.

They decided to do a couple of trials in the hallway the next morning, before entering The King's room.

Shankon poured himself half a glass of wine and Granger joined him at the table.

"I still don't understand why you left the kingdom," Granger said. "You'd beaten the dragons, hadn't you? The people must have loved you. And you left all this?"

Shankon studied his wine for a long time, and finally took a sip.

"I think it's time for you to learn about your parents," he said.

Chapter 14

Franklin's Rules

S hankon set a fresh candle on the table, reconsidered his wine, and topped off the glass.

"Your grandfather was my older brother," he said, looking directly at Granger and speaking deliberately, the way a schoolboy recites his lesson. "Your own lack of siblings lies at the heart of this tale I'm about to tell, so I'll take a moment to illuminate the relationship I had with Franklin.

"He was handsome and well-spoken, with a wit and easy manner that instantly won the hearts of strangers. In short, he had all the qualities that I knew I lacked and I both adored him and nursed a jealous hunger throughout our childhood.

"He never lorded his gifts over me, but the one trait where I rivaled him was stubbornness."

"Was my father like him, then?" Granger the Elder interrupted, eyes intent as Shankon's.

"Presently, presently." Shankon waved and seemed to take a moment to find his place in a text that only he could see.

"To my mind, my brother's failing was that he was too bound by procedure, where I longed for adventure. We shared a fondness for a certain cat, a striking creature with an exotic coat and the air of an aristocrat. According to Franklin's rules, we would provide the cat with a bit of fish or chicken at a regular time each day, lest it abandon us for better hospitality.

"But I thought, why not let him get a little hungry so that he'll catch a rat—they were plentiful at the time—and we'll reward him with the fish. That way, we would enjoy his company, and suffer fewer vermin to boot!

"Franklin had enough years on me that his way always prevailed. As we grew older, he wanted to check the progress of the crops, while I longed for the sea.

"On the day I finally set off to pursue my studies we had a quarrel over some little thing—to be honest I can't remember what it was. Probably something as trivial as how to feed a cat. But where we'd always mended our differences quickly, now we were separated for years, and urgent news cannot travel beyond a messenger bird's range."

Shankon's eyes had drifted down to his wine glass. He lifted it. "To Franklin," he said.

"What happened?" Granger asked. Though it was past time for bed, he stayed alert to every word.

"What happened was I dallied around the world and buried my nose in books and spent time with people not worth remembering. And when I finally returned, I learned that my brother had died several years earlier, the victim of a tree he had felled in the woods.

"He died because of a tree?" Granger thought Shankon must be teasing him about such a serious matter.

"It was not the fault of the tree," Shankon protested. "He was always looking for a better way to do things. He reckoned that once his axe reached a certain depth, a team of four mules hitched to a line around the tree's lower limbs could bring it down and save him a good number of strokes.

"By all accounts, they were exceptional mules and would hold steady until they heard his whistle or the end of the world, whichever came first. But when he took a spell and inspected his work, a badger flew from the brush, knocking him down as much from the shock as the force of the frenzied creature.

"Franklin was tired from the day's work, and dazed by the attack, so he thought he would lay there a moment, collecting himself. But the badger covered the ground to the mules in no time, climbed the tail of one and leaped on the back of its companion, then savaged the pair of mules in front before disappearing in the forest.

"The mules could not help but break their vows, and bolted in four directions, jerking against the ropes that sent the tree on its earthward journey. According to a nearby timberman who was alerted by the awful sounds coming out of the mules, Franklin seemed to lack either the strength, or the understanding of the machinery of fate, to save himself.

"The tree came down with sounds akin to thunder and lightning, with him beneath it."

Granger's mouth became a perfect "O", but no sound came forth.

"Don't ration your strokes, young man," Shankon said presently. "That's the lesson to it. Give the job as much as it requires."

Shankon took a sip from his glass while Granger furrowed his brow in thought.

"And yet," Shankon said "adhering to that lesson may have been your father's downfall. He cast prudence to the wind, and may have sacrificed himself because of it."

Shankon stood and stretched his arms, paced around the table to restore circulation to his legs after the long day.

"And that is the story I'll tell you next, dear Granger. But perhaps it's best left until morning."

Granger beat his fist on the table—quite out of character. "Sit down. And talk."

Chapter 15

A Family Arrangement

This is the story of Granger's parents, as related by Shankon. Franklin named his own son Granger, and that progeny would become known, briefly, as Granger the Elder when he passed his own name to his son, the child Shankon had tried to guide through his early life.

But since Granger the Elder befell an awful fate when his son was but an infant, Granger the Younger never came into currency as a name for the child.

Granger the Elder himself had been an infant when Shankon departed on his travels, so Shankon could not claim to have known the lad. But on Shankon's return, he sought out his brother's son, now in his majority. They met at The Elephant's Tusk for ale and plates of succulent lamb, favored by mint, with turnips and black raspberries by the side. Shankon made theatre of arranging to pay the bill beforehand, while pretending not to be doing just that, so he had a head start on winning the young man's favor.

"You little know me, and I little know you," Shankon admitted. "But your father and I shared that bond of brotherhood that reaches beyond these meager horizons." He swept his arm towards the tavern's window. "And so, I'm offering myself up to serve as whatever inferior shade of a father I might be for you."

Granger the Elder pulled back from his lamb bone and

tilted his head. "What am I to make of that?" he asked. "Who can have two fathers?"

"But that's just it," Shankon cried, slapping the table. "At present, you have none. I could restore at least a part of that deficit."

Granger the Elder looked around the room, at the variety of his neighbors, laughing and eating and cursing and drinking, each to his or her own purpose. A serving lad slipped in a puddle of beer, crashing down with his tray of dishes and the room fell silent for a moment. Then whistles and cheers, boisterous jokes quickly filled the void.

Granger the Elder looked back up to Shankon, and Shankon saw his own brother's eyes looking back at him. "So what are the terms of this contract?"

Shankon waved both hands. "No, no. It is not a contract. Perhaps I could fill a need in your life. A father provides council and support, and in the best cases, the wisdom of experience. I make no claim to be the best possible father for you—because that one is gone—but surely I would be better than nothing?"

"I have not made an announcement yet," Granger the Elder said. "But maybe I can confide in you, as a prospective father. A sort of audition."

"Surely. Go on." Shankon nodded with what seemed even to him as a bit too much enthusiasm.

Granger the Elder took a deep swig from his mug, put it down, and then decided on another gulp before he continued.

"I will soon marry my sweetheart, Geneva," he blurted out. Seeing that Shankon nodded and did not burst into laughter, he went on. "We hope to raise a big family. So no doubt, I will need some fatherly advice from time to time."

Shankon thought it best not to bring up the fact that he actually had no children of his own, and that his wisdom in these matters was derived from observation rather than object lessons. Instead, he raised his mug.

"She must be a most remarkable woman to have smitten you." They clinked pewter to pewter and laughed. "And you are fortunate to have found a woman so remarkable as that!"

"But may I still call you 'uncle'?" Granger the Elder asked. "It sits better on my ear."

"Of course, of course."

"I still don't understand, though." Granger the Elder furrowed his brow. "What benefit this function has for you?"

Shankon's rhetorical skills were celebrated in the farthest reaches of civilization. It was said that more than once the Reaper had arrived on his doorstep, but that Shankon, with nothing more than his words, had beguiled the Old Shadow to cast his scythe in another direction.

Yet he was honest to the core, just the trait that would send him to exile, self-imposed or otherwise, years later. And when there was no profit in persuasion, he favored the blunt instrument of the truth.

"As we grew up, your father, being older, usually had his way in matters, even over my objections," Shankon said. "But even so, I felt that I tempered his most prosaic tendencies. When I left, there was no one present to call him a hide-bound fool, or a blinkered Luddite, or a drudge without dreams.

"I sometimes flatter myself that had I been there, I might have shamed him out of those vanities he chased in the woods. Counting strokes of the axe when there was a life to be lived? My god, he was so much better than that!"

Shankon slammed his fist so hard that ale spouted over the lips of the mugs and left the scent of yeast on the table. Granger the Elder pressed his shoulder blades back in his chair, eyes wide.

"You do flatter yourself," he said at last. And each took the measure of the other for a long moment before they clanked their mugs again and drank to a new relationship.

Chapter 16

Dragons to the Dragon

B ut what was he like?" the younger Granger wondered that night in their apartment in The King's castle. "I can feel him, but I still can't see him."

"Granger the Elder was a bold young man, quite unlike Franklin in disposition," Shankon answered immediately. "He could weigh a situation in an instant, whereas his own father would fuss around and re-calibrate the scales three times before making even a trifling decision.

"But he shared his father's dark hair and striking features." Shankon paused to study the boy's face. "And I can see that you favor both generations in that way.

"Franklin was proud of Granger the Elder, even though they'd endured many disagreements about what path Granger the Elder should take in this or that matter as he was growing up. Along with their physical traits, they both wore a streak of stubbornness. It's not uncommon for the new generation to rebel against the old. You've always been an agreeable lad, but you will no doubt be discovering that for yourself before long."

"Was he tall?" Granger asked, hope cracking his voice.

"A head taller than me, and I'd been level with his father," Shankon said, pulling himself up from the table, stretching to full height and flattening his hand above his head by way of illustration. It took a moment to straighten his knees and back after sitting so long. And then he found he had to catch his breath before going on. "He was easy to spot in the market square.

"Of course, a tall man cannot accumulate debts because he cannot hide from his creditors. In fact, he's denied all manner of sins afforded to shorter folk because any victim of such a sin could easily track him down. Perhaps a man's stature enforces a proportional virtue. To be sure, a greater percentage of the scoundrels I've encountered have been as short of heart as they were in height.

"Stand up now, young man."

Granger scooted his chair back and stretched his spine to the fullest height he could muster while Shankon eyed him up and down.

"You might not realize this," he said, in a tone that signaled an important lesson, "but a tall man must even take special care with the hygiene and grooming of his nostrils since the public, looking up from lesser heights, cannot help but inspect the result.

"So remember, Granger, things that appear advantageous, may be a burden to the one who bears them.

"But I digress."

Granger nodded.

"Later on, your father's stature lent his men spine as they held back the onslaught of dragons," Shankon continued.

"How did he fight the dragons?" Granger found this subject more intriguing than nose hairs.

"With every weapon and tool that fell to hand, and an elastic courage that stretched to contain ever growing dangers."

And so Shankon related the history of Granger the Elder's quick ascent through the Dragon Defense Battalion.

Shankon himself had leapfrogged the royal advisors, landing ever closer to The King's ear. He had his detractors on the court and in the wider society, to be sure, but as he advanced, they brandished their barbs less and less in public. He knew all too well, that only strengthened their private resentments, but that was not the story to be told tonight.

So by the time Granger the Elder and Geneva were to be wed, Shankon was able to secure them a lavish ceremony in the courtyard. The King himself waved from his balcony, and toasted the couple, as striking and winsome as any The King had seen in all his dominion.

"Your nephew and his bride seem like paragons," The King, not given to flattery, said to Shankon a few days later when Shankon offered insight on a question of whether toll gates should consider an ox and a horse equally. Each had the same number of feet, but the ox had twice as many hooves as the horse. That debate had raged on for generations, and, indeed, had sparked minor wars.

"You are too, kind, My King. But I must admit they are a striking couple, and thoroughly mannered and engaging when you make their acquaintance."

"He seems a tall young man, and from his posture I can see good character. What is his position?" The question might have been a trap, but The King showed only curiosity, a rare condition in the royalty.

"Like his father before him, he is a steward of the land," Shankon said. "He brings food for our tables, and wood for the people's houses and furniture. Dear Geneva labors with him in all things, and also supplies flowers to the finest florists. In fact, I believe that is her handiwork by your side."

The King breathed in the lovely scents of the roses, snapdragons and goldenrods in the crystal vase, and swooned.

"But their only goal in life is to be of service," Shankon concluded. "For the betterment of the kingdom."

And that simple exchange—whether innocent or not even Shankon could not say at this late date—led to The King enlisting Granger the Elder to muster forces against the dragons several years later.

And now, as a weary Shankon explained it to young Granger, "We can see the good and bad fruit a certain action might bear, and decide accordingly. But sometimes, our decisions bear a chimerical merging of the sweet and ill that we mortals could never have predicted.

"Some of our actions play out over such a length of time that we lose the trail of cause and effect."

Granger seemed to be frustrated by Shankon's explanations.

"What happened to my father and mother?" he demanded. "How did they die?"

Shankon's eyes fell to the table and he drummed his fingers slowly for some time. Just as Granger was about to speak again, a look of anger warping the cherub's face, Shankon said, "They became hero and heroine to the entire kingdom, and many a dragon regretted their acquaintance."

But he saw no softening of Granger's frown, so he pressed on.

"Their stories will be told beyond my lifetime, or yours," he said, standing slowly again to begin pacing around the table. "Songs of their deeds will be set to stirring melodies to be shared on a special day each year so long as the kingdom shall thrive."

Shankon saw a glimmer of progress in the boy's face and posture.

"A holiday, not unlike Arvon's Day, will be declared in honor of your parents."

"But what happened?" Granger persisted.

Shankon felt his heart sink, and paused again to gather his thoughts.

"As with Arvon's Day, sometimes the inspiration outweighs a clutter of facts."

"Shankon!"

"Very well, then." Shankon considered sitting down again—he was tired enough to do so—but thought better to keep pacing. "Granger the Elder and Geneva called on their troops to chase a dozen dragons into a certain cave, just a few miles from the castle itself. But in the end, they alone had the courage to rend the darkness.

"In the foul air of that catacomb, their final glory was written by flashes of steel and fire, and in the end no survivor, either mortal or lizard, emerged from that cursed hole in the rock.

"In the military calculus, it takes six men to defeat a single dragon in combat. Granger the Elder and Geneva turned the equation upside down. They became dragons to the dragon.

"May their memory long endure." And Shankon turned, as if suddenly admiring the flowers by the window, so Granger would not see the water of his eyes.

Chapter 17

The Audience

Shankon expected breakfast trays when he opened the door to the page the next morning. Instead, the young man, hardly older than Granger, doffed his feathered cap and bowed to the waist.

"Pray be it that you prepare yourself for The King, good sir. He expects you in the time it would take his swiftest horse to make three laps of the city below."

"And how long would that be?" The answer eluded Shankon both for his drowsiness on the one hand, and his ignorance of the speed of The King's horse and the circumference of the city on the other.

The young man twisted his head around on his neck in the unnatural manner certain small birds have of looking at a fresh distraction. "Very soon, sir."

"So you'll send us to The King with our stomachs growling so loud he won't hear our petition?" Shankon sounded incredulous even to his own ear.

"My lord, I have no agenda, only my mission." The page's eyes and the corners of his mouth betrayed his alarm. "And my knowledge that failure in this mission will have consequences more serious for me, than for you." he went on. "You seem a merciful man, good sir?"

Shankon sighed. "Very well." And in a much louder voice, "Granger! Our time has come!"

They dressed quickly as the anguish in the page's face showed the passage of time as clearly as the face of any clock.

The three of them burst into the hallway, with the page looking back, urging them to keep up. Shankon, in particular, walked very slowly at first, but as the blood began to flow again in his legs, he began to make pace. Granger, for his part, walked abreast of the page.

"You know, the fault lies not with you," Shankon said, as he regained his air, "But with the one who sent you on an errand without sufficient time to complete it. Have no fear, good man, I'll argue your case with The King. What is your name?"

"I am Winton, son of Karamus," the boy said, looking over his shoulder in near terror now. "But it was The King, himself, who sent me."

Shankon never missed a stride, neither from the shock of the identity of the boy's father, nor that of his dispatcher. "I see," he said. "You must trust me to smooth the waters for you, just as we trust you to deliver us to The King's throne."

Granger the Younger marveled at the immensity of the castle, and all the twists and turns through its unmarked corridors that their guide traversed with ease.

"Your father helped bring us to the castle," Granger said.

"That was but the first step in your journey," Winton said, sounding a little dismissive to Shankon's ear. But Shankon could well understand the tone, as it related to Karamus.

At last they arrived at sixteen-foot double doors, each with a strapping attendant, clad in crimson and wafting perfume, who manned the door ring.

"Permit us a moment to rehearse our presentation," Shankon said to Winton, as Granger stepped to his side to practice the kneeling ritual they'd gone through before.

"Alas, I cannot," Winton said, nodding to the doorsmen,

who grabbed the rings over their heads and labored through arcs to pull the doors into the hallway.

And there it was!

Granger had never imagined such a sight. They stood at the threshold of a great hall, its walls lined with murals in silk and velvet, torches blazing at each buttress. Busts of all The Kings past gazed out from pedestals that flanked the entry carpet, each one looking remarkably similar to the one before it. Granger had heard parables of The King with a Thousand Faces. Here were a thousand Kings with One Face.

And at the far end of this aisle rose a throne on a platform six feet above the floor of the great hall. And behind it, a reticulated window that illuminated a thousand points of dust as it bestowed a halo on the man on the throne, who must be The King.

As they walked along the plush aisle, Granger felt as unsteady as Shankon had seemed when they rehearsed this scene in their apartment. But now Shankon strode forward in bold abandon, shoulders thrown back, wisps of white hair flowing back from the fringes of his scalp, while Granger scrambled to keep up.

It seemed to take forever, and in one corner of his heart, Granger wished that it would take forever, for he could imagine no thrill greater than this. But at last they reached the spot where the carpet had been worn thin by the knees of earlier supplicants, and Granger took his cue.

Shankon began to lower himself, gently taking Granger's shoulder for balance, as they'd practiced. But after their meandering through the castle, Shankon's knees seemed to creak louder than before, and he took both of them down in an unceremonious heap.

Granger found his bearings more quickly and helped Shankon up so that they could both kneel properly before

The King. Granger somehow hoped against hope that their little disaster had not been noticed.

"I am Shankon, My King," Shankon announced in a loud, clear voice that surprised even Granger. "My ward and I have answered your summons."

"Indeed you are, Shankon," said The King in a voice that Granger could not parse. The sound of it was reedy, uncertain, as if forced from the royal throat. Shankon's voice, on the other hand, flowed from deep within his soul, resonant to every ear, when he was on his game like this.

"But before we get to my service to The King, I must address the matter of Winton, son of Karamus, who escorted us to this hallowed place."

The King sat silent, and with the light behind him, and Granger's fear to look too closely, Granger could not make out what he might be thinking.

At last, The King spoke. "You realize that the kingdom is once again in dragon peril, and that our very survival is at stake?"

"I do," Shankon said, head bowed.

"And yet you want to discuss some matter relating to a page?"

"I do," Shankon said, nodding.

The King fell silent for what seemed like an eternity to Granger, but was actually only a few breaths.

"So! What is it?" he barked at last.

"It seems that Winton was dispatched by a fool who did not allow enough time for the lad to complete his task. Therefore, I submit that any consequences of his failure of a timely deliverance should fall on the dispatcher, rather than the underling facing an impossible task."

"But I was that dispatcher!" The King shouted, a little less reedy this time.

"As I am aware, My King." Shankon rose up from his

knee. "And I am here because you beckoned me. But when you seek counsel you must heed counsel. My advice in the case of Winton is to credit the lad, for he performed miracles beyond his years in stirring me to action before the breakfast which you denied me.

"If we do not treat our fellows in the kingdom with dignity and justice, how better are we than the dragons themselves? We have our dungeons and chains, they their flames and death. But what difference is there, really, for their victims and ours?"

Granger was coming to understand that The King was not especially quick of thought, and he felt his breath catch at least twice as he awaited a response.

"Shankon," The King said at last, "Years ago, you said many things to me that would have resulted in a head on a pike at the castle's gate if they had come from any other mouth.

"And I see that you have not changed. In fact, I know that you will never change, which is why I called for you. I'm surrounded by buggers whose only goal is to divine what I want, so they can parrot it back to me.

"My father warned me of the royal life, yet he offered no remedy!"

"And so, Winton is absolved?" Shankon pressed his business.

The King waved his left hand. "It's nothing."

"So then, when shall Granger and I have our breakfast?"

Chapter 18

Breakfast Choices

While Shankon and Granger fell on their hunks of stag, roasted with coriander and peppercorns, The King sat across from them at the breakfast table, now and then popping a raisin or fig into his mouth.

"We saw peasants gathering the dragons' stones and dung from their fields," Shankon said. "That will be a good start for feeding our cannons."

The King seemed distracted. "Hmmm? Yes. I suppose so."

Shankon sopped his bread in the pool of stag juice. "But what is this nonsense we hear about a dragon circling the city as we were on our way here?"

The King stopped snacking and looked glum. "It is true."

"But how can that be?" Shankon had been hoping for a different response.

Granger, who'd gathered that bit of intelligence himself, pursed his lips and shook his head.

"While the flock gathers at the headwaters, they are sending scouts to plot their return?" Shankon asked, feeling his stomach knot around the breakfast he'd so far consumed, even though he'd known all along that this would be the explanation he dreaded.

"And it is even worse than that!" The King looked gloomier by the moment. "Each day, two or three of those winged abominations have been harassing the mines that yield the ore we need to forge the cannons. The peasants fear those foul beasts more than they fear my own wrath!

"'At least The King might be capable of mercy,' they say. Well, there will be no mercy when I find out who spread such a damnable lie about me!" He pounded his royal fist so hard on the table that Granger's knife bounced off his plate.

Granger grabbed the knife as it wobbled, but then was uncertain whether he should restore it to the plate, or rest it on the table. The one thing he knew was that he didn't want to draw The King's attention, so he slipped the knife under the table and tried to become absolutely still, invisible, while this older generation sorted the matter out.

"Past dragons were simple beasts, driven only by their hellish—and predictable—impulses," Shankon was saying, neglecting his meal. "But just as they've honed their death skills in each new emergence, now it seems they have advanced their higher faculties. They are able to plot and scheme, harnessing observation and logic for their foul ends, blind to empathy and bent solely on destruction." He shook his head mournfully. "We have lost our advantage."

"So you're saying all is lost?" The King cried. "My Kingdom is lost?"

Granger realized he'd been holding his breath. All at once, he needed so badly to suck in a bushel of air, but such a spectacle would betray his invisibility. So he let the oxygen seep in quietly through his nostrils, just enough to keep from exploding, not quite enough to satisfy the needs of his lungs.

"The kingdom need not be lost," Shankon said, stepping away from the remnants of breakfast, and pacing clockwise around the table, his hands clasped behind his back. "We still have more experience with our brainly functions, while our adversaries are no doubt given over to sophomoric reveries inspired by their newfound skills. Mankind invented chess. These wretches have only just noticed a pattern to the board."

"Then what shall be done?" The King seemed to brighten a little.

Even Granger, callow as he was, thought The King's moods too easily swayed. He much preferred Shankon's calmness, even in the face of danger. Who could predict which way The King might twist if presented with conflicting views?

"You must, by royal edict, delegate all authority in dragonly matters to me, so that a workable plan can be developed and executed with neither the duress of committees, nor dissent of the ranks," Shankon laid it out, front and center.

And The King blanched. He, too, stood, and began pacing, counter-clockwise, hands clasped behind his back.

"There are certain considerations," he croaked, clearing his throat.

"Politics!" Shankon grew impatient. "Isn't that exactly what spoiled our last stand against these monsters? Didn't the fools trifle away our time, palming their daggers, lurking there, waiting for their chance?

"And now we're back at our starting point, but with a more meager arsenal than before.

"In fact, I seem to recall that I was brought up on charges when the very thing I'd predicted—that the dragons would escape to terrorize another day—came to pass precisely because of our political disarray."

Both men stopped and glared at each other from opposite ends of the table.

"I granted you a full pardon!" The King's weak, tortured voice seemed even more wounded now.

"Which I would not have needed if you had only granted me the powers I now seek. Those same powers you denied me at that time."

Each man resumed his journey around the table, and as they passed each other, twice in each circuit, their eyes fell sidelong on the other. Shankon kept to the inner lane, and they both stopped in their tracks and faced each other again when he spoke.

"I need your answer," he said. "And in this instance, I find myself strangely aligned with our cursed foes. For the dragons await your choice with all the eagerness that I do. Only they hope for the opposite outcome."

The King flopped his arms in his robes and shook his head beneath the crown. "You understand there are considerations—"

"Exactly!" Shankon shouted. "You are considering the difference between life—or at least the chance of life—and death."

The King leaned against the table looking weary, although the day was still young.

"Will you take an audience with the Archbishop? I'm sure you'll win his favor, and he can evangelize from there."

"Shall I meet him before or after the court jester?" Shankon's stomach was beginning to grumble.

"I can still have your head on a pike, you know!" The King's words were more fearsome than his tone. And then even his outline seemed to deflate. "It's a simple formality. Just explain the situation to him as only you can do. Ten minutes and you'll have him."

Granger counted to twenty before Shankon replied.

"Very well. Send a fool to meet a fool. I see that it makes perfect sense."

The tension lifted from the room and Granger was able to breathe freely at last. He jumped up from his chair and waved his hands over his head, one of which still held the knife.

"I know you well enough to know that you always have an alternative plan in case of failure," The King said to Shankon. "But I never would have guessed that you were grooming assassins."

He nodded at Granger and they all broke into laughter.

Chapter 19

Persuading the Archbishop

This is a good omen," Shankon whispered to Granger when a page cried the arrival of the Archbishop at the door of their apartment, scarcely an hour later. "He at least recognizes the urgency of the situation."

Their discussion was cut short as their visitor filled the door frame. He let out a faint grunt as he ducked his head and entered. Granger was relieved to see the big man doff his brown, velvet cape. The garment had a mink collar, with two mink heads lingering in a rodential kiss beneath the Archbishop's chin. Granger didn't think he could have maintained his own decorum for long if he had to look at that.

"Shankon, it has been a long time since we last met," the visitor declared.

"Indeed, it has," Shankon said, waving toward the wooden chair at the other end of the table. "Won't you have a seat?"

"Thank you, yes," the Archbishop said, sinking deep into the plush sofa. "I trust you've lived a godly life during your exile?"

Shankon took his seat at the table, and Granger tucked into his own chair. "I have continued to live true to my nature," he said. "If there is a more godly way, I know it not. And, frankly, I am beyond the desire or the need to learn new skills."

"I see you have not changed," the Archbishop nodded, as if he might be about to drift off to sleep. "And The King has treated you well?"

"Who could quibble with The King's hospitality?"

The big man laughed, and for a moment, Granger might have thought the two men were friends.

"Only one who has not enjoyed its full measure, I'm sure, dear Shankon. He has always found a softness in his heart for you. A whisper from your lips to his ear becomes law." The Archbishop's words seemed sporting enough, but Granger saw no humor in his face.

"And yet," Shankon said, "there is a royal craving for your blessing."

"I have no blessings to bestow," the Archbishop countered, stroking his beard, but keeping his hard, glinting eye on Shankon. "Those flow from a power beyond mine."

"Nevertheless, The King feels that your good word with the powers that be could finally unite the kingdom in this critical time."

Granger had once thrown his neck out of joint by watching a spirited badminton match, turning this way and that with each volley of the shuttlecock. He feared that the crimp was about to return this morning.

"Perhaps the time has come to state your case, Shankon."

So Shankon laid it out at length, and Granger felt the tension in his neck ease as he settled in to listen.

Shankon sketched the history of dragons, of their ever-growing danger with each generation, and of the causes and results of the kingdom's failure to eradicate them in their previous cycle.

What's more, he detailed the mathematics and physics behind his vision for using the dragons' own dung and stones to power the cannons that would destroy the beasts. And once the cursed army was defeated in flight, Shankon would oversee the destruction of all dragon eggs remaining in their lairs to eradicate their future threat.

The Archbishop pressed the fingertips of one hand to those of the other, forming a perfect little church steeple beneath his chin—where not so long ago those minks had been kissing. He breathed in and out so deeply and noisily, that across the room, Granger might have taken it for snoring.

"And so, Shankon, you think this plan—this rational plan—will be more effective than the holy prayers we can offer up throughout the entire kingdom? We have an inexhaustible supply to be issued over days, weeks, months, even years!"

Granger thought it sounded like this was the first time the Archbishop had ever said the word 'rational.'

"What remedy have those prayers achieved in the past, your Grace?"

"What remedy?" The man nearly rose from his cushion, but thought better of it. "How much worse things would have been without those prayers!"

Shankon stood, clasped his hands behind his back, and began circling the table, as he had earlier that morning with The King.

"Movement restores circulation," he said to the Archbishop after his first lap of the table. "So the blood can do God's work."

He paced a little more and then came up short, standing straight and true, projecting the forceful voice Granger knew so well.

"You have told us many times how God granted mankind dominion over the earth and all its fruits, and all its creatures."

"I have, for that is true."

"But you have also told us that He finds us wanting. We yield to our petty temptations, pray for mercy, only to yield again."

"Such is the nature of mankind. And the nature of infinite mercy."

"Aye, but what if that mercy has its limits?" Shankon clasped his hands again and resumed his pacing. "Wouldn't prayers that go unanswered be proof of such limits?"

The Archbishop's face darkened, but he remained silent. To Granger's eye, he didn't know how to counter this argument.

"And perhaps the Master of the Universe has grown so disenchanted with our recalcitrance that He thought better of giving mankind dominion over the world? Perhaps He bestowed that on another species, one unfettered by our weak morality? Who would alert us to this change in the cosmic plan?

"Who but the dragons themselves?"

"Stop it!" The Archbishop launched himself from the cushion, and the heavy couch skidded across the floor from the force of his departure. "This is blaspheme!"

"Indeed?" Shankon stood his ground. "Then which way do the scales tip? Is the penalty for blaspheme more or less harsh than actual subservience to this spawn from hell?

"From where I stand, your cure is worse than the disease." Shankon was usually spare in his gestures, but now he waved his arms wildly. "Better to perish trying to vanquish evil, than play into its hands by sending our petitions of mercy into the void!"

"Blaspheme!" the Archbishop cried once more, before he stormed out, slamming the door.

The breath heaved in and out of Shankon for a full minute, but to Granger it seemed like an eternity. Then Shankon ran a hand over his balding head, patting down the vagrant wisps of hair, and plopped down next to Granger.

"That probably didn't go as well as it might have," he said, winking.

Chapter 20

The Magician's Offer

Shankon had not used a quill in some years, and he found it tiresome trying to consign his thoughts to paper. So he requested—and promptly received—another audience with The King in advance of the afternoon's meeting of the Royal Council.

This time Granger stayed behind, where he cringed when he realized that in the Archbishop's hasty retreat, he had left his hideous cloak behind. So Granger rolled the garment up, hiding the heads of the minks in several layers of fabric, and left it on the couch.

When Shankon returned after some time, the furrow of his brow had smoothed, and the hint of a smile teased the corners of his mouth.

"So, what happened?" Granger asked, when he could stand the suspense no longer.

Shankon explained that The King had been engaged in a meeting with Morganthal, The King's personal magician, when he arrived.

"An odd duck, that one," Shankon said. "I think you would have liked him. He would have you believe that birds and flowers are the same thing. And before he's done with you, your eyes would believe it, too."

Granger grew impatient. "Yes. But then what?"

"Well, then he offered spells that could be used in defense

against the dragons. You know, his apprenticeships are the most coveted in all the kingdom. Apparently there is some glamour attached to his position. In any case, he is able to secure the best and brightest youngsters to form an army of assistants. And those neophytes soon learn to cast spells sufficient to deter the dragons. Or so he claims.

"I had to laugh and tell him that he sounded quite a bit like the Archbishop. One wielding prayers and the other incantations, and each as likely to be turned into a cinder on first acquaintance with a real dragon."

Granger waved his hand. "Yes. But then what?"

Shankon shrugged. "Well, I was not turned into a toad, if that's what you mean."

"No!" Granger cried, letting his frustration get the best of him. "About The King? About the Archbishop? About the Council? About the dragons?"

"Oh, that." He nodded, pretending to take Granger's meaning for the first time. "Well, The King had hoped to call on the Archbishop to address the assembly today, to win them over as some sort of independent voice. I will grant that he would be independent, for the Archbishop's interests and those of every other soul in the kingdom have no points in common.

"But in light of the Archbishop's tantrum, we'll press our case to the Council without him." Shankon tilted his head. "You look worried, lad."

"Didn't The King think he was needed to win the Council?"

"Indeed. But I convinced him otherwise, just as I will convince the Council that the Archbishop's position is fine and good, and totally irrelevant. After all, we have the arrows of truth and logic and science in our quiver."

Even Granger could see that those weapons might not be up to this task. After all, for years in the wilderness, he'd listened to Shankon's tales of the ineptitude and folly of this very Council.

But Shankon stretched his arms and announced, "So I believe I'll take a short nap, to restore myself before this afternoon's meeting."

And he plopped down on the sofa and immediately sprang back up with a cry, clutching his buttock.

He'd landed on the rat-like teeth of the Archbishop's cape. He shook the fabric until the taxidermist's handiwork revealed itself.

"Spies!" Shankon declared. "This is but a timely reminder that we can never let down our guard, neither with the dragons, nor with their agent, the Archbishop."

Granger felt he might be liable for rebuke for having set the booby trap, but the mood Shankon brought back from his meeting could not be so easily spoiled.

"While I take my rest, you can take this rag to the stables that some mule might find comfort in it," he said. But he grabbed Granger's wrist before the boy could leave.

Shankon loosened his purse strings and shook out a handful of coins.

"Have Winton, Son of Karamus, gather some of his fellows and pay them with these for a certain service they might render..."

In hushed tones, Shankon laid out the tasks to be performed, and then drifted off to sleep while Granger made the arrangements.

But memories of past Council meetings haunted Shankon's dreams.

The Council of The King has always had three major factions.

First, there was the Ancestral Party, comprised of nobles and successful merchants whose philosophy holds that their fathers, their fathers' fathers, and so on had arrived at a perfect government, so any changes to that structure would inevitably be for the worse.

Next was the Children's Party, made up mostly of serfs and peasants, the common people who proposed common-sense reforms that might leave a better world for their progeny, and indeed for the entire kingdom

And finally, there were the Pragmatists—known to their detractors as the Fantasists—who dedicated themselves to incremental change by forging compromises with the other two parties.

In his previous encounters with the Council—it seemed like a lifetime ago, though in fact less than a generation— Shankon felt a kinship to the Children's Party, as well as an affinity for the Pragmatists. So he was able to build a popular consensus in most matters.

But neither reason nor charm chinked the armor of the Ancestrals. In rare cases, he could sway one member or another from his party's doctrine with outlandish flattery, but in most cases, even this passed over them as lightly as a summer breeze, as if no compliment lay beyond their due.

So Shankon came armed with popular opinion, but often was defeated because Horace the Archivist ruled that it was written that the Ancestrals' votes weighed half again as much as the will of the other parties.

Horace had held this position for upwards of fifty years. In those times, a man might accept the Reaper's tap, grudgingly, but accept it nonetheless, at age forty-five. So few citizens, let alone members of the Council, could call back a time when Horace was not the sole authority on the documents in his keeping.

Rather than some vast library, Horace played guardian to only two broadsheets of parchment.

The first, the Holy Writ, detailed the sacred laws and the means of their enforcement. This had been laid out by a forgotten scribe with an ear to God's Lips, and consecrated with the passage of time. On rare occasions, the Archbishop visited Horace to consult in these matters.

The second was the Ancient Draft of Authority, which described the powers of The King, the Council and the Church, the lines of succession, the rights of taxation, the avenues of petition and other principles of civil government.

Horace alone in all the living kingdom had read these documents for, as he frequently attests, the ancient media are so exceedingly fragile that even the over vigorous blink of an eye might damage the parchment.

So the kingdom, both Church and State, rely on Horace's memory of these documents, although he freely admits he has refrained from consulting them for decades precisely because of that fragility. And Shankon was not alone in noting that Horace's recollections of these writings, as well as his memories of the day's breakfast, seemed as precarious as a dandelion gone to seed.

Horace has drawn a modest salary for his service to the kingdom, but his unique position has earned him invitations to the royal banquets, and confidential deliberations that no other civil servant enjoys.

And indeed, his fine clothes and enviable accommodations would seem to beyond the reach of a man of his stature.

And thus the stage was set for Shankon's dream that noon, ahead of the Assembly.

Chapter 21

Shankon's Dream

In his dream, a younger Shankon, with so much more to lose, looked out from the dais at the Council. They stared back impassively as the feathers in their hats waved in the breeze created by rock-muscled fan men who heaved in alcoves at the pulleys that drove the great, cooling sails that stirred the air above.

The members were seated at their desks in neat, concentric semi-circles. The position of each one told an intricate story of ambition, compromise, survival and failure. Even in his dream state, the tragedy struck Shankon that a man's whole life and worth could be plotted by his place on the axes of the Assembly Chambers.

He was due to brief them on the latest news from the dragon front, but when his turn came, he found he could not speak.

The words scrabbled in his throat, like desperate moles seeking darkness. He looked out in growing horror, but his eyes found no safe harbor in the cold faces that ringed him.

Shankon coughed, as if the labors of the sweating fan men had drawn dust down from the rafters to fill his lungs. He doubled over, nearly retching, before he finally gathered himself. He blotted his tears on his sleeve and finally croaked, "I come to bring you news of the battle."

But before Shankon could continue, a sharp rebuke rang

out from the gallery. Sir Gregory, chief delegate of the Ancestrals, leaped to his feet and pounded his desk, sending a spray from his inkwell to the floor. "How dare you speak of news?" he thundered, "When you bear the oldest story of all, the story of our humiliation in the face of reptilian evil?"

Shankon was accustomed to Sir Gregory's outbursts, but this seemed off the mark, even for him. The words echoed off the walls, as if they'd all been whisked from the seat of government to the dank grotto of despair. And again, Shankon lost his tongue.

So Sir Gregory plowed ahead, turning from his spot at the very center of the inner circle to address his colleagues with a great deal of waving arms and flying spittle.

"Indeed!" he cried. "The gentleman has capitulated to every demand of the dragons. Up to and including—" he turned back to aim an arthritic finger at Shankon—"the sacrifice of his own nephew on their altar of evil!"

A collective gasp rose from every throat, which decayed into a muted babble, not unlike the sounds of an orchestra's final tunings before a concert.

And from there, Sir Gregory shouted on, waving in a conductor's frenzy to control the pitch and cadence of his instrument while Shankon watched, dumbstruck and diminished.

"...under penalty of death!" Sir Gregory concluded, and the 'ayes' thundered around the dome of the Assembly chamber, while Shankon struggled to understand what had befallen him.

And then, in the manner of dreams, Sir Gregory became a human veneer draped over a dragon's core. His face shimmered, poorly concealing the lizard within.

"Do you see?" Shankon cried out to the Assembly, regaining his voice at last. "Don't you see?"

But before his answer came, Shankon found himself alone on a vast beach at low tide. He'd visited such places often in his travels as a younger man, but their mysteries seemed just as fresh now.

Overhead, the sky was clear, and a cooling breeze, not unlike that generated by the fan men, came off the ocean. Thunderheads rose over the distant waters, teasing the roar and fury they might soon bring to shore.

The bubbler crabs had thrown up their sand balls in perfect, concentric circles that spread across the beach before him. And Shankon could not help but think of the precise geometry of the seating chart in the Assembly Chamber. The crabs had laid an intricate lattice of tiny mounds of sand in a pattern beyond the reckoning of their own feeble minds.

And at the changing of the tide, all that was beautiful, and all that was inscrutable about their creation would be laid to waste, only to be laboriously reconstructed as the waters ran out again.

In his dream, Shankon saw the same patterns. Humans waxed and waned in relation to the dragons. Civilizations flourished and civilizations perished in cycles that outstripped the reckoning of either man or lizard.

How was Shankon any more significant than a bubbler crab molding a few grains of sand against the force of the ocean? How could the bickering Assembly strive for any greater place in history than a nest of crabs? Are we not just Sisyphus on the beach?

Shankon might have been hit by the violent wave of the ocean's oblivion when he jolted out of his dream.

Indeed, he was soaked, although not in salt water, but sweat, as he emerged from that dream world to that couch, in the apartment they'd been allowed in The King's castle.

Granger was shaking Shankon's damp shoulder.

"It's almost time," he was saying. "Won't they be waiting for you?"

Chapter 22

The King's Speech

It was unusual for The King to spare time from his kingly endeavors to sit in on a session of the Assembly, but there he was, surveying the proceedings from within the purple velvet drapes of the royal box at the head of the gallery.

He lifted his opera glasses and scanned the very heart of his government. "Clerks!" he snorted to Lady Thwarte, who shared his box. "Sticky-fingered louts! Mewling children who have lost sight of their good fortune."

"Indeed," Lady Thwarte nodded so enthusiastically that her wigs threatened to topple from her head. "There's so much to be learned from the olden times. You could rule by decree and dispense with this circus."

Since their marriage, it seemed to The King that Lady Thwarte's voice had dropped a register. What once seemed a seductive whisper, was now an annoying rasp. And she'd slabbed on a little weight, year by year while The King himself seemed to be slimming by an equal measure. Their total weight remained the same, but its distribution shifted ever her way.

O, and she had been a frivolous thing when they'd dallied in the buttercups, just a flirt and a joy, coaxing him out of the cloak of dread he wore at the thought of ascending the throne, and what an awful responsibility that would surely be.

But now he had grown capricious in his rule, while she had turned dour as the Fates, spinning their final skein.

The King shook his head. "I don't even know what I would decree if I reclaimed that power," he said. "Youth's clear vision becomes murky with time."

He turned to look at her and Lady Thwarte's expression prompted him to go on.

"Yet, your beauty remains a constant through the ages."

She worked her fan more vigorously. "I don't see why you can't dispense with the sniveling class and rule like a true king? What is it that scares you, Your Highness?"

"'Your Highness?'" he threw it back to her. "How long has it been since you've called me by my rightful name?"

"Very well, then." Lady Thwarte tilted her head back as if she might balance an egg on her chin. "Why don't you cast out these fools, Your Folly?"

The King clucked and sighed. From the royal box, they could spy on any member of the Assembly, but no member dared look up for fear of meeting the royal gaze. So, the presence of The King dampened the rowdiness of the usual political discourse.

"Look!" The King pointed to a figure in a white robe striding to the podium. "It's Shankon's turn."

Shankon took his place and laid his hands on the stand and seemed to draw resolve from the inlaid panels, worn smooth by the grip of a thousand orators. He had been one of those speakers and now he would be again.

Later on, he would confide in Granger that he may have been the first ever to return to that hallowed station after falling out of favor. Because the loss of esteem was usually accompanied by the loss of some vital organ or another, heart, liver, spleen or brain—the mob would accept any of these tokens, but nothing less.

So Shankon had barely opened his mouth, when applause

rang out from all the far walls of the Chamber. Granger, Winton and Winton's many confederates clapped and cheered, prodding the Assembly, ever fearful of being out of step, to join in.

And as Shankon completed each thought, the applause rang out again, starting from the far walls, and pulsing through the crowd in a crescendo. Granger called out, "Hear! Hear!" in a voice so comically deep the crowd might have turned in laughter if it hadn't been such an integral part of the general din.

It little mattered what Shankon actually said, but he laid out his plan to save the kingdom, indeed, mankind, earnestly, transparently. He caught himself feeling humbled by the ovation, even though he knew those few coins he'd distributed through Granger to Winton had purchased this response.

"And so, I put it to you," Shankon said, summing up at length. "Won't you delegate those discrete powers to me, on behalf of your constituents, your families, and your own mortal souls?"

This time the applause continued so long that Shankon's mind began to wander. He thought of how stiff and weary his legs seemed, and he leaned this way and that against the podium to find some relief.

At last the noise died down and Shankon nodded to the President of the Assembly, and walked back up the aisle to take his seat in the visitors' section of the Chamber.

The President of the Assembly shambled up to the podium and studied some papers. "We have heard Shankon's argument. Do we have any further debate before we vote on his resolution?"

Five heartbeats passed, but just before the gavel fell, Sir Gregory stood in the innermost row. "Shankon has been most eloquent in his appeal," he said, in a tone that dripped rancid oil. "But beyond his ad hominem attacks on the dragons—"

Shankon shot to his feet in the back of the room, surprising even himself at his spryness. "Have we sunk so low that we must listen to apologists for those deadly lizards in this revered place?" he cried.

Sir Gregory threw his arms in the air, an injured supplicant, and the President of the Assembly bellowed, "You had your time, Shankon. And now this is the other time."

"Thank you," Sir Gregory said, brushing his hand over his breast as if he'd found some crumbs after a meal. "As I was saying, even if we could get beyond the questionable philosophy, the strategy and tactics and unforeseen consequences of the honorable man's master plan, we would butt our heads against the wall of the Ancient Draft of Authority.

"This whole, grand scheme runs counter to the Ancient Draft on points of conscription, taxation to underwrite the crazy enterprise, preservation of exotic species, abrogation of authority—the list goes on and on.

"So I would suggest we call Horace the Archivist to testify to these contentious issues."

A groan rose from the crowd, even louder than the applause Shankon had enjoyed during his presentation.

"Perhaps that won't be necessary," the President of the Assembly said.

And in the royal box, The King felt Lady Thwarte's elbow strike his rib. He jumped to his feet and addressed his body politic.

"No, that will not be necessary," he said, as every ear strained upward.

"A King's fate, envied perhaps by those who have not endured it, is to rule over all things. But even a King cannot know all things, for such universal knowledge is beyond our mortal tethers.

"Yet we humans, with great diligence, may become proficient in one aspect or another of this brief, precious prize that we call 'life.'

"The dragons have dragged us to a new frontier where questions of biology, ballistics and battle tactics dot the horizon. Shankon is my guide to that terrible frontier. And he will be your guide as well."

The King looked out over the Assembly and saw that he had their full attention. Their eyes locked on his robes and crown. No cough nor sneeze nor short breath broke the silence.

"I grant that Shankon's art of persuasion can sometimes take flights of fancy."

Shankon stood and waved from the back of the Assembly.

"But that is the price I pay for safe passage through this hostile frontier," The King went on. "And that is the price you shall pay, too, my countrymen."

The King did hear a short breath, but it came from Lady Thwarte who was regarding him with a look of respect he'd long forgotten. He bowed to his people and regained his seat.

The President of the Assembly whispered among his aides for some length of time. He cleared his throat and banged his gavel.

"No further vote shall be required on the motion," he declared. "Let it be written that the authority sought by Shankon is hereby granted, and its exercise shall be the law of the land."

He rapped the gavel one more time before the first shadow crossed the Chamber's stained glass window, and the awesome call of monsters rang through the courtyard.

Chapter 23

A Vision of the Future

Follow the guards!" the President of the Assembly cried, with another rap of his gavel. "And we're adjourned!"

He took the gavel with him as he fled. Whether for defense, or from habit, who could say?

The guards, calm and practiced, led the Assembly and the visitors down spirals of stairs, through great wooden doors that slammed shut behind them, ever deeper into the catacombs beneath the castle.

Shankon, like some of the older politicians who jostled around him, felt short of breath as their pace picked up. They ran down this hallway and that set of stairs, past inscrutable doors.

It occurred to Shankon that this might all be a plot of the Archbishop, that their final turning would land them in a dungeon, never to see natural light again.

But at length, the guards ushered them into a great room, remarkably similar in size and furnishings to the Assembly Chamber that they'd fled.

Granger found a high perch and watched in amazement as each politician was drawn to his place in the Chamber, like filings under a magnet's pull.

Shankon saw Granger clinging to the buttress and bade him gather his mates and join him on the gallery floor.

While the Assembly collected their thoughts and waited

for the President to rap the gavel again, two guards approached Shankon.

"You must come with us," the taller guard said.

"To what end?"

"To satisfy The King's orders."

"Very well." Shankon had regained both his breath and composure. "And to give The King even greater satisfaction, we'll bring my band of young soldiers along."

The guard gave his fellow a puzzled glance. "We have no instructions beyond you alone, sir."

"Then consider this the appendix to those instructions," Shankon nodded. "The King loves children, for they are the future."

The guards shrugged at each other and they led the entourage on another complicated journey. They wound through so many corridors and entries that Shankon lost all reckoning of their actual location.

At last, they were deposited in a lavish office where The King sat on a high pedestal, with Lady Thwarte examining her nails in the flicker of the sconce on a slightly lower platform.

"Your Highness," Shankon said, waving his arm in a broad arc. "I expect you enjoyed a shorter passage than we, your humble servants."

"You know that I cannot confirm that," The King said. "Nor shall I deny it, for reasons that I don't even recall at the moment. And which seem irrelevant, in any case.

"The important thing is, you are here in safety." The King arched an eyebrow and continued after a beat. "With your ragamuffin army?"

"With my precocious ward, Granger, whom you've met," Shankon laid a hand on Granger's shoulder, and swept in the rest of the crowd. "And Winton, son of your loyal servant Karamus, and his stout warriors who have vowed to defend the kingdom to their last breaths."

Shankon didn't look, but he knew, and Granger later confirmed, that each of the lads grew fierce, for their honor had never been defended—never even been imagined—before.

"So," Shankon said. "You rely on my knowledge, but at the moment I expect your knowledge of our current predicament is greater than my own?"

The King held his gaze and said, "If it were a kingly thing to feel shame, then that would be my feeling now.

"But it is not, so I will simply tell you that thirty, or perhaps two score, adult dragons are circling the castle. It's hard to get an accurate count, the way they swarm through the sky. They are belching flames at the spires, but so far no direct attacks on man nor beast has been reported. Similar tactics are being used on the city below."

Shankon stroked his beard as Granger looked up at him, as expectant as The King.

"So this is a mission of reconnaissance or intimidation, but not an actual battle?" Shankon asked. "Is that your meaning?"

"So it would seem," The King said. And Lady Thwarte glanced briefly away from her nails to Shankon beneath her.

"Then we have a far graver emergency than you have described," Shankon said, his voice stirring in that way that always made Granger look up.

"In what way?" The King remained oblivious.

"In that your agents have gathered intelligence that has not been available to me!" Shankon jumped up so quickly, shaking his fist at The King that the guards, who had been loitering nearby, wondered for an instant if The King were in danger.

"Indeed," The King admitted. "And that would be the source of my shame, if such were my lot."

"My King, My King!" Shankon's head sank. "How can we

mount a defense when our sentries are cut off from their generals?"

"If I were your equal, I would beg your forgiveness," The King said, quickly feeling the slap of Lady Thwarte on the back of his head, before Shankon looked up again.

"We once faced human enemies, when words might win a war as easily as swords," Shankon said."But what is this place, where the enemy flaunts intelligence? An enemy that assesses the battlefield and develops strategies and tactics, without a common tongue?

"Would the incarnation of Death itself look any different than this foe? Conscience, mercy, compassion, remorse— these are just words, and words ring hollow on a dragon's ear. We've entered a barren battlefield, and I scarcely recognize it."

"Come with me and we'll see what we can see," The King said, leading Shankon and Granger toward an alcove in the far wall. "Lady Thwarte will deal with the rest of your party."

In the alcove, they strapped themselves into a gilded cab. No sooner were they secure than the cab began to rise up as somewhere in the walls, servants sweated over enormous gears, winching them ever higher in the darkened shaft.

For a long time, they rose slowly, rocking in the cab. Granger peered into the darkness and whispered, "I can't see past my toes."

"There is nothing past your toes," Shankon said, and immediately realized this was not as comforting as he'd intended. But he said no more.

Abruptly, the ceiling creaked open above them and light streaked in, playing off dust that danced like fairies in the shaft. They emerged on the Great Parapet, an outpost that commanded a view of all within the castle's walls. With a glass, one could assess the city below, as well.

Even before they took in those sights, Granger, Shankon

and The King felt the sting of sulfur in their noses, and their eyes watered with the smoke.

But even for the tears, they all saw a terrible future taking shape beneath them, as if they were the first guests arriving at the terrace overlooking hell.

Chapter 24

The Dragons' Advantage

Each year, the share of the population of Shankon's age seemed to dwindle, both in numbers, and influence. His contemporaries were dying off, regardless of their station in life. And their experience seemed less and less relevant to the new generations that crowded them out.

But to the last, Shankon and his aging brethren would testify that the current situation seemed bleaker now than ever before.

"Not long before my time on this earth, people of the same age I am now, told of times before the dragons had even mastered flight," Shankon had often remarked to Granger. "Bookmakers did a brisk trade in the square wagering on how many nestlings would break their necks on the rocks beneath their lairs.

"And now those monsters have perfected that skill, along with a host of new ones."

Over just a few generations, the dragons' breath perfected itself from the hot stench of swamp gas, to the occasional burst of flame, to the cyclonic torch that could now lay waste to a village. Indeed, in the early days, the hatchlings had been so clumsy that they might incinerate the whole of their broodmates.

"Strategy? What's this talk of strategy?" Shankon had muttered in his sleep, awakening Granger. "They're animals! How would they employ strategy?"

And now Shankon leaned over the Great Parapet, The King on his right, and Granger on tip toes, at his left. They wiped the sting from their eyes until the tableau resolved itself beneath them.

The courtyard seemed drained of color, save the yellow glow of the fresh dragon dung, and the orange flames that traced the outlines of things that might have been men, or horses, or some other beasts.

On the other side of the wall, blackened fish and frogs floated, polluting the moat. In the distance, they saw smoke curling up from the village. None of them dared take the glass to that scene.

And from within and without the walls of the castle, all was silent. No bird called. No insect buzzed.

No mourner cried out in anguish.

"This is not the end of the world," Shankon said at last.

"No?" The King seemed surprised, as if he'd been hoping at least for some finality to cling to.

"Not so much the end, as its aftermath." Shankon pulled Granger fast to his side.

They breathed in the foul air a little longer before Shankon remarked, "I thought you said they were merely scouting, leaving few casualties?"

"Aye." The King shook his head with a sadness unbecoming of royalty. "I will see that my sentries are punished for the failure of intelligence."

Shankon snorted and waved at a pair of gray silhouettes charred into the cobblestones below. "There's little you can do to them now," he said. "Perhaps the Archbishop can suggest further measures."

"Damn you, Shankon! I am The King, and I would tolerate such talk from no one else. Your fate is in my hands."

"Exactly," Shankon nodded. "As yours is in mine, by the look of things."

The King took several deep breaths through his teeth, as if those could filter out the sulfur fumes, while he surveyed the charred remnants of his realm.

"Very well, Shankon. What are we to do?"

Shankon let go Granger's shoulder and made a quarter turn to face The King directly, his feet planted, shoulders straight, his voice dropping to a minor key.

"First, we'll need a census of the dead. Inscribe their names on marble tablets at the castle's gate. Declare three days of mourning, to be followed by an annual holiday to rival Arvon's Day, during which their sacrifices will be honored. Pay an annual stipend equal to half again the victims' wage to the widows and orphans, or to the husbands for those women who were taken."

To Granger's eye, The King seemed to have turned into a wax mask.

"Ye gods, Shankon! How much time will that take? How much will it cost? Don't we need to raise an army?"

"You'll have your army, and it will be loyal to the last, if you do these things," Shankon said, with some patience. "If you do not, you might as well send a courier with the key to your bedchamber to the dragons' lair."

"But the price is so high! There's so little time!"

"True enough," Shankon nodded. "But consider this: The dragons have always been defeated, and they have always returned. Perhaps young Granger can explain this to you in simple terms."

Shankon nudged Granger forward and he glanced up, halting at first, to meet The King's sad, brown eyes.

"The dragons might eat this man or that, but that meal does not satisfy their hunger," Granger said, as if the words came from some place beyond him, maybe near the Great

Parapet's ceiling. "Because they feed on your fear, not your flesh. Each time they reappear, they are sowing the fear they will reap on their next appearance."

"I told you he was precocious!" Shankon patted Granger's shoulder and swatted his own thigh.

"I swear, you infuriate me, Shankon." The King walked the circumference of the parapet, muttering to himself.

"Your Highness, surely you remember that fine stallion you had so many years ago? I believe his name was Royal Shade?"

"Remember him? Who could forget such a magnificent creature?" Granger thought The King considered such a question to be bordering on an insult.

"Indeed, the straight and true cannons, the arc of his hip, the flare of his nostril, the penetrating eye," Shankon ticked off the attributes, "those would catch the breath of a horseman in his throat."

The King shook his head slowly, the mist in his eye having nothing to do with dragons now.

"And those were the same features Granger and I recognized in the horses that your men, Lawrence, Karamus, Paramus and Daramus rode when they fetched us to your court.

"How could it be that a horse long gone has made such a mark on your royal stable today?"

The King looked at Shankon as if this crazy old man had just fallen out of the sky. "Are you such a fool?" he cried. "I bred the best mares in the kingdom to Royal Shade, and the outer kings sent their finest stock to him as well! He left a mark for the ages!"

"Precisely!" Shankon said. "And I would submit that the dragons have an understanding of husbandry as lucid as your own."

"Have you gone mad?" The King's eyes darted to Granger

to see if the boy was hearing the same nonsense that he was.

"Not at all." Shankon gazed toward the mountain tops, where the smoke was already dissipating. "In the past, men made sport of the dragons' bumbling attempts to fly, to breathe fire, to conjure a battle plan. But so what if only one in a hundred survived those bold attempts at advancement? If ninety-nine were doomed by wings too feeble for flight, one passed on its endowment.

"Those dragon cocks and hens that survived laid a new baseline for the next generation. And their progeny proved ever more deadly to our race."

The King paced more quickly. He waved his hand in front of his face, as if trying to pull a certain word from his mouth, then flung both hands overhead in frustration. A few guttural sounds echoed off the ceiling of the Great Parapet.

"Yet where are we?" Shankon wondered. "A dragon generation is considerably shorter than that of mankind. And, in any case, what improvement in the nature of man could the historian point to over a span of ten or twenty generations?

"Privilege and class and tradition dictate our breedings, which is why we are saddled with monstrosities such as Sir Gregory and The Archbishop. The dragons, for their part, rely on utility alone."

The King, looking weary, planted his hands on the rail and looked out over the once-green fields to the smoldering city. Thrice he sneezed, rapidly, from the lingering smoke and sulfur.

"If you were a painter, Shankon, you would be a pauper," he said at last.

"I tell you what I see because I lack the skill to render it on canvas."

"So whatever is to be done?" Granger had never even thought about a man being broken, but to him, it seemed, The King was a broken man.

"We are still smarter than the dragons," Shankon said, in that same reassuring Shankonesque voice that had shepherded Granger through his childhood.

"Though perhaps not for much longer."

Chapter 25

The Dragon's Hearing

When The King pressed his seal to the Royal Statement Concerning the Delegation of Authority in All Matters Pertaining to the Current Plague of Dragons, Shankon was at last able to get to work.

He sent an expeditionary force, flying no flag, but carrying a loft full of messenger birds, up the valley to discover and relay back word of the enemy's location and activities.

He installed Lawrence, his one-time escort—or captor!—at the head of a task force to arrange the necessary compensation of the surviving families.

He tripled asbestos production and sent troops to provide cover for the iron miners who now suffered frequent hazing from the dragons. The foundries worked night and day, producing cannon barrels.

He dispatched an army of peasants over the freshly soiled land to gather the explosive dung and digestive stones left by this latest raid.

And Shankon himself lobbied the Assembly to resolve the debate that had stymied him in his previous sojourn with the court, so many years ago.

When Shankon had arrived in the kingdom after his youthful travels abroad, there was great discussion over the relative merits of catapults and cannons. Both weapons could deliver a payload with similar heft, over a similar range, although the cannon held the edge in accuracy, if operated by a skilled team. And indeed, the cannon needed fewer men to deliver a blow.

The catapult camp argued that their device was easier to manufacture, and relied on the muscles of men to wind the lever—calculated as a zero-cost item in those days—rather all that fussy business with procuring gunpowder and fuses.

"With its greater accuracy and more efficient use of manpower, the cannon is clearly the superior weapon for this struggle," Shankon had declared, his voice rising in the Assembly Chamber all those years ago. "And in addition to those advantages, the roar of the cannon itself will strike fear into the dragons."

Predictably, Sir Gregory took the floor.

"We all want to rid ourselves of this curse, but this is a specious argument," he cried, flinging his hands to the vault of the ceiling. "Dragons, like their serpent brethren, have no ears, so how could they hear a cannon's retort?

"And besides, a dragon fears nothing!"

"Then speak to this, Sir Gregory," Shankon came back, with a cock of his head. "If dragons have no fear, why do they transform themselves so in each new birthing? Why indeed, if not to escape some mortal danger?"

Shankon and Sir Gregory haggled over the matter until the Assembly became restless in anticipation of lunch. So the principals devised a test. As Shankon pressed his case, Sir Gregory asserted that not even a catapult was needed: even a sling could fell a dragon just as well.

Their compromise was that Sir Gregory would send one of his aides, a young man who had won slingmanship awards in recent Arvon's Day contests, to the Great Parapet. Once there, he would taunt a circling dragon to test its hearing. And then let fly his stone to demonstrate that he could bring it down.

To Shankon's eye, the lad seemed not yet out of adolescence. In any case, the youth's confidence fell short of Sir Gregory's as he took up his mission.

"Hey, dragon!" he cried from the Great Parapet. "Over here!"

For its part, the dragon never even deployed its flames. It simply plunged from its great height, swallowed the aide up with a great gulping sound as the lad's boots were sucked in, and disappeared into the sky in a single arc.

"I'll grant you they have some rudimentary hearing mechanism," Sir Gregory shrugged. "But I maintain that the sling is an adequate counter-measure. It was not properly tested in this case."

Shankon felt overcome with nausea. "You sacrificed that dear boy for your vanity?"

"A pity, isn't it?" Sir Gregory feigned concern. "But his nerve failed at the crucial moment, so how long could he have lasted in any case? I have other aides. And more will join my office in the years ahead.

"You and I, Shankon, must take a larger view, to be masters of this game."

And now, years later, Shankon couldn't help but wonder if he'd let his disgust with Sir Gregory weaken his resolve at a crucial moment. While Shankon tried to rally the kingdom against the dragons, Sir Gregory and his band of scoundrels in the Assembly pitted their strength against Shankon. In any case, appropriations bogged down, and the kingdom had lost its advantage by the time the cannons finally roared. Countless lives were lost, including those dearest to Shankon.

And so here they were, Shankon and Sir Gregory, sizing each other up in the Assembly chamber.

Sir Gregory clapped a hand on Shankon's shoulder in the manner of old friends. "It has been a long time, Shankon," he said with a smile so incongruous with the glint in his eye that Shankon stepped back and barely suppressed a gasp.

"I see you have no dagger, Sir Gregory. Haven't you replaced the one you left buried in my back?"

"Be a sport, Shankon. It was never personal. We all do the things the things we must do. All my actions, then and now, have been in service of my constituents."

Shankon brushed the scaly red hand off his shoulder. "Then and now, I have dedicated myself to making the dragons suffer," Shankon said. "You want to offer them suffrage."

Sir Gregory leaned back and let out a galling laugh. "You always had a way with words, dear man! Perhaps you could negotiate your settlement with them."

Shankon shook his head slowly, but held Sir Gregory's beady eye. "I see it now," he said. "The fire-breathing hellions are fierce, but short-lived. They rise up to dominate mankind, but once they've done their worst, they die off, and our race ascends once more. It's the cycle of dragons: Evil traces its arc through the sky, until we're able bury it once again. And dance on the brimstone to seal the grave. Perhaps that is the cycle of politics as well, and we pray that your cause shall soon be turned to ash."

Sir Gregory's jaw twitched, and he was the first to blink.

"Perhaps I overestimated you, Shankon." And he gave a grimace of a smile. "But I'm late for a debate on the budget."

He tapped his forehead and let his palm fall between them to bid farewell.

Chapter 26

Running the Board in Bokan

Granger's heart rose when Shankon proposed a round of bokan. They hadn't played since they'd left home, and while life in the castle brought daily marvels, just the mention of bokan flooded him with excitement, nostalgia—and a lust for victory!

But on the crest of that wave, came overwhelming guilt.

"Do you have time to play, with everything you need to do?" he asked Shankon.

Shankon suppressed a laugh. "I daresay I've managed my time much longer than you yours," he said. "Yet we've both reached this place without regrets over trifled moments. Game on?"

That was all the convincing Granger required. He set the board with quick, precise moves and bounced back in his chair in anticipation.

The fact was, Granger had known few children of his own age. He'd learned what he knew of conversation, housekeeping, the physical sciences, humor and the art of bokan from his interactions with adults. And his talent for bokan outstripped his prowess in all those other categories.

By the age of eight, he'd been hailed as a fourth-degree master. With a preternatural eye for strategy, he could translate the pips on a die into a ruthless offense, pressing ever deeper into his opponent's heart. Bokan was the most serious and ancient game in the kingdom, but Granger flung over the table of the old masters' theories.

"Now, are you sure you have time for me to beat you?" Granger asked, once the board was cast.

"When faced with insurmountable problems, it sometimes helps to consider a different challenge altogether," Shankon said. "In this case, how could an old fool like myself ever hope to outwit a prodigy on the bokan board? But the challenge frees up the mental juices, the better to digest the original problem."

So Shankon rolled the die and made his clumsy opening.

Granger looked up to see if this move was a joke. He shrugged, rolled his die and claimed an unsatisfying victory in five moves.

"Two out of three?" Shankon ventured.

"We don't have to play," Granger said, unsatisfied by such an easy win. "You might not be at your best tonight."

"Surely you won't deny me the honor of a full set?"

Granger sighed and let Shankon lay out the pieces on the board. Granger played a conventional opening, but Shankon countered with a move so random that Granger came up short. He studied it from every angle. Surely Shankon's ploy had some underlying logic—but whatever it was seemed impenetrable to Granger.

"People think this game is named for its inventor," Shankon said, while Granger studied the board. "The scholars have debated that without resolution. Where they have found consensus is that it is the oldest game. What could be more elemental than advancing your stone across the board, against all opposition, to meet its goal?"

Granger frowned and waved his hand impatiently for Shankon to be quiet. Shankon's first move gave him no advantage and left him open to attack. How many moves ahead was the old man planning? Granger needed to find the logic so that he could counter it.

"But beyond the simplicity of the play, there are so many layers of symbolism," Shankon kept droning on. "Your marker can be a stand-in for a religious mission, a twist of philosophy, a moral universe that you're compelled to impose on your neighbor. A flat, worn stone becomes proxy for all the hubris that has plagued mankind down through the ages.

"So was Bokan the man who invented his namesake game? Or is bokan just a manifestation of the human condition, rendered in wood and stone, with the die furnishing the chaos that rules our lives?"

Shankon watched Granger fretting over the board for some minutes before adding, "What do you think?"

Granger slapped the table. "I don't know. I don't know. I don't know. Why did you make that insane move, Shankon?"

"Play it out and see." Shankon leaned back in his chair.

Granger stared at the board three minutes longer before he, too, leaned back in his chair.

"I resign," he said.

Shankon rested his elbows on the table and clasped his hands above them.

"And why is that?" he asked. "You're much the better player."

Granger snorted. With his own eyes, he'd seen Shankon defeat six masters in a sweep, prowling the aisle from one table to the next.

"I couldn't see where you were going, so how could I know what to do?" Granger tried to keep his voice even, but even he felt he might be whining.

"And what did I tell you at the outset?"

Granger's face contorted. "What?"

"That putting the focus on a fresh challenge frees the lower mind to answer the original challenge."

"I don't understand? What was the purpose of your move?"

"You'll never know now, because you didn't play the game out." Shankon let his hands cradle his chin now as he leaned forward again. "You let your fear of the unknown prevent you from winning.

"But in fact, the move was not a lesson for you, but for me."

"Sometimes I hate your riddles!"

"The dragons have their rules. The Assembly theirs. The scoundrels, the Archbishop and the Sir Gregory's and their ilk, their own. It's up to us to devise the rules we need to win the game."

Granger's face began to light up for the first time that evening. "So you didn't know what you were going to do next yourself?"

"Oh, that would be telling," Shankon said. "Now, two out of three?"

Chapter 27

Progress and Peril

From the Great Parapet, Shankon and The King could watch the preparations advancing on every front. A thousand laborers fortified the walls of the castle, as did two thousand more in the city below. Carpenters boarded all but strategic windows as their hammers struck a staccato refrain.

Shiny, oiled cannons that had never been fired were wheeled into position, and the smoke from the foundry in the valley promised more would soon join them.

The rapid thud of arrows peppering targets echoed off the walls as the archers perfected their skills. Columns of infantry slashed and blocked, applying sword and shield to an invisible enemy.

The scents of burning sage and cedar mingled and rose to their perch.

The King turned his gaze from all this industry and fixed it on Shankon.

"So, are you confident in these preparations?" he asked.

"It's not a matter of confidence," Shankon warned, planting his hands on the rail, still looking out at the activity below. "Confidence implies some measurement that must be achieved to seal the day. And that in turn implies some limit on what we must do.

"Would a man cast at sea reckon some number of strokes he could endure before succumbing to the water? Or would

115

he swim to the very last fiber of his being? Just so, we cannot be satisfied by any less than all we can give. Failure earns no appeal in this battle."

The King snorted. "Did you know the Archbishop accused me of listening to you because you offer false hope?"

Shankon laughed and waved at the archers below. "A bowman with the Archbishop's record of accuracy would soon find himself in the infantry."

The first birds were returning from the scouting parties that were making their way toward the headwaters where the dragons traditionally took their spell before attacking. Shankon told The King that the spies reported smaller knots of dragons forming, perhaps a few dozen in each location, scattered up the river that had so far been surveyed.

"Damn you, Shankon! What does that mean?" The King demanded.

Shankon smiled, further inflaming The King. "In the past, the dragons have always launched a single, massive assault. And they have always been repelled, with a greater or lesser cost to our side.

"This new pattern could mean that they will launch a less virulent but longer lasting war of attrition."

"My god! What shall we do?" The King clasped his breast, as if stricken by a wayward arrow from below.

"We shall let me finish, in the first order," Shankon said, shaking his head slightly enough to avoid agitating the sovereign any further."This might also mean that, like our archers, infantry and cannoneers, they are breaking into units of specialized talents, foul as those might be."

The King gasped, but Shankon plunged on. "Or it could be that the resources they need to sustain themselves through the battle are lacking at the headwaters, so they are spreading their numbers along the river merely to survive."

The King sighed deeply in relief, but Shankon still went

on, "Or it could be part of a greater strategy that we have not enough information to recognize."

Another royal gasp.

"Your Highness," Shankon said, "I find it beneficial to take several deep breaths, to truly exercise the diaphragm, in order to moderate one's reaction to the pendulum of fortune. Whatever will be, panic never wins the day."

Just then, an arrow clattered off the ceiling of the Great Parapet and landed at their feet. Shankon leaned over the rail again and surveyed the field below.

"Good news, Your Highness! We have a new infantry-man!"

The King was not amused.

"You know, Shankon, every day people tell me you an unserious man with a private agenda. One who not only should be ignored, but should be banished back to the outer realms whence he came."

"And those people would be the Archbishop and Sir Gregory alone?"

"No! There are several more. Sometimes even Horace the Archivist joins the chorus, but I can't imagine what his interest is."

"Be it remembered that I returned from the outer realms not by my own initiative, but under escort of your guard, and at your whim?"

The King's hands fluttered, as they often did when he did not want to be bothered. "The point is, Shankon, that I've underwritten your every whim. If the enterprise fails, how does that reflect on me?"

"In the words of your fair Lady Thwarte, 'No action of The King reflects on him, for he is the source of the light'"

The King screwed up his face. He didn't recall Lady Thwarte ever saying such a thing, but it sounded true to character. His hands fluttered some more.

"Very well, Carry on," he said, striding for the gilded cab. Taking his seat, he pulled the sash to be lowered back into the bowels of the castle.

Shankon took his seat on the bench to wait for the cab to return. He felt hope from the progress that had been made. At the same time, he felt despair at the folly of The King, the intransigence of Shankon's political foes and, yea!, even at the wiles of his ultimate, reptilian opponents.

It was exhausting work, suppressing both human folly and hellish fury at the same time. And time grew short.

Perhaps the clock had run out on mankind, and the time had come for Homo sapiens to succumb to *Ignis spirans draconis*.

Shankon, who had not shed a tear since the loss of Granger the Elder, planted his eyes in his palms and wept freely for the fate of his Granger the Younger, the kingdom, and even the ridiculous King himself.

At length, the gilded cab returned. Shankon sat in it. He pulled the sash and felt gravity ease him through the depths of the castle.

Even as the messenger birds brought news from afar, Shankon also had sources closer to home. Young Winton and his crowd of pages, messengers, laundry maids and servers discharged their duties as invisible as sprites. Their work ensured life ran smoothly in the castle. They provided grease to the gears of government. Indeed, the kingdom might collapse in chaos without them. Yet few of their masters could put a name to one of them.

They might have been invisible, but to Shankon, they had ears of gold, eyes of crystal. And to Shankon they were loyal to a fault; not because of the few coins he had circulated among them, but because he learned and remembered their names, and the details of their lives they shared with him.

So it was only natural that they also shared the malignant

schemes and petty crimes of the nobles, politicians and frauds to whom they catered.

Chapter 28

The Dragon Hedge

So many wild thoughts—conflations of memories and dread—revolved through Shankon's dreams that he could scarcely cobble enough sleep to contain the images on any given night.

He woke—or had he even slept?—at first light with a catch of breath. In a moment, he recalled where he was, and the tasks that faced him. He went to the pot and the water bowl for his morning ablutions. He sat at the table for some time with his hands clasped, although he issued no prayer.

The birds were conversing outside, so he flung open the window to the perfume of lilacs as the sun broke horizon beyond the city.

Shankon tapped Granger's shoulder and whispered his name.

"Mmmm?"

"Granger, let's go for a walk in the topiary, before the heat of the day robs it of its pleasures."

This might not have been Granger's first choice of activity, but he'd been abandoned to the solitude of these quarters so much of late, that he jumped from the bed, clawed his hair into some kind of order, and was ready to go in an instant.

They strolled among the shapes of lions and elephants, the creatures of distant lands. Shankon seemed lost in con-templation, but Granger marveled at the sheer audacity of this garden. The natural bushes had surrendered in service of some greater power. The result seemed at once beautiful and terrible to his unschooled eye.

"Shankon?"

"Hm? Yes?"

"How do these shrubs grow into these shapes that belong to other things?"

"They don't grow in such a manner," Shankon laughed. "No more than a child's whims and fears haunt him into adulthood.

"Rather, the topiarist envisions this world and bids his army of gardeners to render and maintain it. Do you like their handiwork?"

Granger thought a long time. "I do," he admitted at last. "But it's also scary. What if we turn a corner and see ourselves clipped out of a pair of shrubs?"

"Now that would be an honor!" Shankon laughed again.

But Granger wasn't so sure. "Or would some part of us be stolen? Would we be the weaker for sharing that outline?"

"You're a curious young man, Granger. That will put you in good stead as you come of age. Curiosity is perhaps mankind's most valuable quality. And perhaps its rarest, as well."

They strolled past the hippopotamus, the fox and the unicorn before Granger asked, "Are there any dragons among these shrubs?"

"I think not, and I am glad for that fact. The topiary should soothe one's temper, and such a monstrosity would have a counter effect."

•

While The King had granted Shankon broad powers, Shankon had been betrayed before. He was hampered by how much he could trust his new delegates now. So he sought counsel in Granger whose friendship with Winton, son of Karamus, opened a door to Lawrence, Karamus, Daramus and

Paramus, the four escorts—or captors—who had brought them to The King in the first place.

Although he'd made sport of them at that time, Shankon respected their honor and dedication to their mission. After their common adventure, he felt he could trust at least those four soldiers.

So, through Granger's connection, he soon made Lawrence his lieutenant of the pending Armageddon. Daramus, whose skill with the pan and herbs had impressed Shankon and Granger on the trail, became quartermaster. Karamus oversaw all mounted troops. And Paramus plotted the logistics of the war to come.

Next, Shankon sought out the parents of some of Winton's gang. They were the ones who had been keeping the kingdom on track for a generation, much more so than the politicians, clergy, and dissipated nobility.

In each case, as Shankon built out his bureaucracy, he mobilized talent all too happy to at last have their worth recognized.

"Our world needs no more speeches," he explained to Granger as they split and shared an orange, drinking in its scent, and lapping the juice that ran down their wrists, that afternoon. "The time has come for action."

While Shankon's agenda moved forward, setbacks plagued every waking hour, and indeed even through the dead of night.

The asbestos mines lagged behind their quotas, likely because the rights holders could contract a higher price by making fanciful projections of their output. Hairline fractures produced by the accelerated schedule, rendered many of the new cannon barrels useless, prone to shattering on first volley.

People were stealing out of the city at night, preferring to take their chances dispersed in the hills. And still the messenger birds brought reports of strange behavior all up the river, knots of dragons swooping like hawks to pluck an ox or an ass from the field.

And still, Shankon had to battle for consensus on even the slightest matters in the Assembly. He went to The King.

"You are a very fortunate monarch, Your Highness," Shankon told him. "You may only have one hundred ten chairs in the Assembly, but with that number, you have two hundred twenty opinions. Perhaps even more."

"You know I don't like riddles." The King seemed irritable these days, which gave Shankon some solace. "Out with it!"

"Each chair represents an agreeable opinion and a contrary opinion, regardless of what the proposition is. And which way the chair votes depends entirely on who whispered last in their ear, or the temperature of the chamber, or whether breakfast took issue with the digestive juices it met.

"How is one to face a mortal adversary with such fickle support?"

The King nodded in resignation.

"You leave me no room to argue, dear Shankon. But some things are beyond even a King's command. The Ancient Draft of Authority is clear on certain matters and I cannot overturn it."

Shankon imagined Lady Thwarte would be as disappointed in this reply as Shankon himself was. But he said, "Have you ever seen the Ancient Draft of Authority?"

"Of course not." The King snorted. "But Horace has. And like my father and his before him, and his before that, I am bound to rely on Horace's telling. Horace is the sole authority in these matters."

"But what of Morganthal the Magician? What happens if his counsel conflicts with that of Horace?"

"It never has!"

"And the Archbishop?"

"Never!"

"And Sir Gregory?"

"I say never!"

"And common sense?"

The twitches of insult, betrayal and understanding at once racked The King's face. "Spare me, Shankon," he cried. "These matters are settled!"

"Settled on the word of a man so old that none alive today can even remember the day of his appointment? One who has never shared the source of his authority? Even the Archbishop and Morgenthal the Magician make more plausible cases than that.

"How is it that the kingdom, and The King himself, have been subjugated by such a whim?"

"Many have told me I should have you put to death," The King—call him The Scarlet King for the flush of his face—said, "Don't give me further temptation to yield to them."

A purple satin pillow struck The King, setting his crown askew, to the amazement of both The King and Shankon.

"You'll yield to no one," Lady Thwarte shouted, advancing into the room with a few, crisp strides. "Have you lived longer than all your ancestors to learn nothing from your reign?"

As The King tidied his appearance, Lady Thwarte turned to Shankon and said, "You'll excuse us while we tend to domestic matters, sir."

Shankon bowed and backed up towards the door where he bowed once again and entered the corridor with a clearer idea of what must be done. And there was a spring in his step, at last.

Chapter 29

The Plans

Winton's army of children handed up frightful, maddening bits of intelligence to Shankon, not unlike a cat dragging the carcass of a mouse to its master's bed chamber. The Winton brigade might have been no more than flickers in the shadows for all the impression they made on the weighty people they attended. But no conspiracy escaped their ears.

That's how Shankon knew that Sir Gregory planned to disgrace him with a vestal virgin that would be discovered in Shankon's bed. That plot seemed to be undone by Sir Gregory's lack of acquaintance with any such candidates.

And that's how Shankon learned that the Archbishop planned to leave noxious traces of devil's toe and ground serpent's tooth about Shankon's apartment. This scheme, apparently, was foiled by the Archbishop's failure to procure these substances outside of his own, personal supply.

So even as Shankon saw hope, his detractors weighed upon him.

Shankon and Granger had been staring so long at the bokan board that they'd forgotten whose turn it was.

"Your move," Granger ventured at last.

"Indeed? I thought it yours."

"It doesn't matter. I'll beat you either way," Granger said without enthusiasm. "Take three moves, if you like."

"I'd best resign then."

"You can quit the game, but then you'll have to tell me what your problem is."

"Where is that written?" Shankon became indignant. "Are you the Horace of the bokan rules?"

"I don't know what you're talking about," Granger admitted, scooting back a little in his chair. "But you can't quit just for the sake of quitting. Wouldn't you tell me the same thing?"

Shankon had to admit as much.

"The problem is hubris," Shankon said, after a brief reflection. "I'm beset by fools who cannot even imagine the possibility that civilization might end. In their memory, and their parents' memory, and their grandparents' memory, even to the next generation, civilization has always been a rock upon the horizon. So how could that ever change?"

As he often did when troubled, Shankon paced out laps around the table.

"The real problem is that the dragons learn from their shortcomings and evolve ever stronger. Meanwhile, men never learn and are trapped into repeating their old follies.

"Most likely, we will survive the current onslaught, which has already begun. But the way their offensive capabilities are outstripping our defenses, or even our awareness of danger, next time, or at least in the span of your life, young man, the dragons will be able to wipe out the human race.

"And what then of the kings and scholars and poets that have sustained us through the millennia? All will be ash, and only the crow of the dragons will ring out."

Still, Shankon was able to shake off his pessimism. In the first wave of reconnaissance dragons, the archers had brought one to earth. Besides the beast breaking its neck on impact, it was a near perfect specimen. The Royal Surgeon and the Royal Taxidermist worked together, both to map the creature's vulnerabilities, and to provide a model for training the troops.

For example, the lap of the third scale from the left wing gave an attacker access to the demon's shriveled heart. It could be slain by no more than a single spear—or even a dagger—if properly placed.

Shankon himself demonstrated the lethal maneuver for class after class of archers, spearmen and infantry, and many of them would soon owe their lives to this single lesson.

With Lawrence and Paramus, Shankon developed the strategy and tactics for the coming war.

The dragons had superior mobility, so most efforts went towards building a strong defense. But they did sketch out some offensive measures. Since the dragons had broken with the past by dividing into smaller groups spread out along the river, they presented new vulnerabilities. Even now, elite bands of soldiers advanced on the lairs, armed with catapults, siphons, and barrels of Greek fire which would incinerate the dragons while they slept.

On the home front, great shields of asbestos and bull leather gave cover to the cannons, archers and spearmen.

When they struck, a swarm of dragons was so thick that the shot of a single cannon might drop half a dozen winged demons. Those that were not killed outright, could quickly be dispatched with the blade techniques Shankon was teaching.

A handful of skilled archers could bring an individual down like a doomed pin cushion. This was a more precise attack, but it also required more manpower per kill.

At least, those were the plans.

And soon enough they would know if their preparations had been adequate.

Chapter 30

The Sermon

Shankon woke at the first call of the bluebirds and threw the sash to reveal the rosy light of dawn. The scent of lilacs and ivy greeted him. It wasn't certain at that moment, but this would be the final Sunday morning before the dragons mounted their offensive.

He tapped Granger on the shoulder until the lad relinquished his dream.

"Come, come," Shankon said."Let's go hear what this morning's sermon is all about."

Granger rubbed his eyes. Surely he must still be dreaming. He'd never known Shankon to care about sermons, and he said as much.

"Not for our edification, although I would never deny you that if you sought it," Shankon said, arranging his garments. "But so many people we will be counting on will be there. We must be aware of the public's state of mind, for that is what our fate turns upon."

It turned out to be a doubly rare day. Shankon made his way to church, and the Archbishop addressed the congregation.

Many years earlier—so many years earlier that their relationship still might have taken a different turn—the Archbishop had confessed to Shankon that he had once loved to speak to his flock. Shankon had not witnessed that, but he had no doubt of it, because in his experience, no sound captured the Archbishop's fancy so much as that of his own voice.

But what the Archbishop had confessed was that he feared running out of words. Just as a man might be allotted so many heartbeats at birth, what if a man's speech would be cut off when he reached that birthright quota.

For one such as the Archbishop, Shankon acknowledged, that might be a fate worse than death itself.

But Shankon also realized that lurking somewhere beneath the Archbishop's apprehension was the awareness that his flock would grow damn weary of him if they had to listen to him prattle every week for twenty, thirty, forty years.

The Archbishop gladly delegated the routine engagements, the sermons, the christenings, the eulogies, counseling, sympathy and all the bloody rest of it to his subordinates. So now when the Archbishop spoke, the flock would prick their ears!

Shankon and Granger found seats in a pew near the back of a packed cathedral on that fine Sunday morning.

Granger looked around, not sure what to expect. But he knew that Shankon still had many obligations to fulfill, with little time left.

"Won't you get in trouble for being here?" Granger whispered.

"The last time I came, we were told that all would be forgiven," Shankon whispered back.

But Shankon remembered previous services tipping the scale towards heaven. As the Archbishop hit his stride, it soon became apparent that hell was on his mind.

"...and so we wait, listening for the roar of the dragons' wings through the valley. And we offer up prayers for protection." The Archbishop raised his arms overhead. Then he clenched his fists and pulled his hands down slowly, as if lowering a heavy curtain. "But what hypocrisy is this? For would we be facing such an awful fate if some among us had not called it upon our heads by forsaking the Lord?

"Look to your left!" One arm darted out. "To your right!" And then the other. "Which of your neighbors threw his lot in with the army of sinners whose deeds we will all pay for now?"

Granger screwed up his face quizzically and tugged on Shankon's sleeve. Shankon's finger made little circles in the time-worn sign of scrambled brains.

"The end is nigh!" the Archbishop shouted. "Ask yourself if your tithes are current! Your money will be worthless in the next life, but there's still time to purchase your passage to heaven."

Unlike past services, Shankon noted that the offering plates remained in constant circulation. He watched with a mixture of dread and amusement as citizens who abstained, or paid a few token copper coins on one round of the plate began tossing out silver on the next pass.

The Archbishop labored for a solid hour, painting a picture not just of imminent doom on earth, but of eternal damnation for all who had not divested themselves of their worldly fortunes. His sweat drew dark shapes on his velvet robes, and he mopped the lather from his brow with one sleeve, then the other. His eyes blazed red with the salt that poured from his body.

Shankon was the first to stand when the Archbishop at last quit the pulpit. He looked around the room to take in a slack-jawed, wide-eyed audience that would need at least a few moments to return to the common realm.

"Well, that was certainly . . . interesting," he said to Granger.

For his part, Granger traced loops in the air with his finger, a gesture that made a great addition to his repertoire.

Shankon had thought to return to their apartment for a

proper breakfast, but a page intercepted them and led them to The King's quarters.

The King leaned back in his cushion and waved to the sofa for Shankon and Granger. Lady Thwarte sat forward on the opposite sofa, one hand across her lap, and the other plucking red grapes from the bunch. She didn't seem to chew so much as suck them down to a pulp, which she swallowed in due course.

"I saw you at the service," The King said. "The Archbishop certainly hasn't lost it, has he?"

"Probably not," Shankon seemed to agree, "unless you're referring to his mind."

"Oh, come, man. The people need a conscience, and he provides it. I can't imagine it's an easy job."

Shankon laughed. "Certainly not for him!"

"Oh bloody, bloody, bloody," The King said, then caught himself and cast a sidelong look at Lady Thwarte who was narrowing her eyes at him, and sucking particularly hard on her current grape.

"So, Shankon. Thank you for coming. And you, as well, Master Granger." The King smoothed his robes as he collected his thoughts.

"Thank you for the opportunity to be here," Granger piped up, which threw The King off balance for another moment. Was Shankon actively coaching this boy to take over his role in the future?

"The King has news from the birds," Lady Thwarte prompted.

Shankon and Granger turned in unison, each cocking his left eyebrow at The King.

"Yes, yes," The King said. "We've had messenger birds coming home in flocks lately. They bring good news . . ."

Lady Thwarte threw a grape that splattered on The King's crown.

"... and some news that's not so good."

Shankon looked at Granger and asked in a stage whisper, "I wonder which he'll tell us first?"

"The good news," The King announced, "is that your scheme of incinerating the smaller groups of dragons in their lairs has been quite effective. Most of the forces closest to us have been dealt with."

"That was the low-hanging fruit, as the saying goes," Shankon said, stroking his beard. "So if a near certainty fulfilled ranks as good news, my heart grows heavy waiting to hear the bad news."

Another grape to the crown prodded The King to continue.

"Well, as we thought, and hoped that we might have several days yet before the major offensive began, it now seems that the flocks are gathering and could be here as soon as tomorrow."

The King looked at his audience to see how the message landed.

Shankon leaned forward with his elbows on his knees and his forehead in his hands, as if overwhelmed by the bad news. In fact, the shield of his hands allowed him to steal a glance at Lady Thwarte, who still did not seem pleased with The King's performance.

"Your Highness," Shankon said, rising back up, with his hands swiping down slowly over his brow, cheeks and chin, "Pray we hear from Lady Thwarte, a wise woman, a wise counsel, who has been privy to the birds as much as your royal self?"

Lady Thwarte made no haste to dispatch her current grape. But when she had swallowed it, she stood and said, "We cannot predict a time with any precision because much depends on how they expend their energies on destroying the crops and villages they find along the way.

"But tonight is likely the last we'll know that is not interrupted by the belching flames and the lingering stench of those beasts.

"As you well know," she looked at The King, although she was addressing Shankon, "my husband has lived far beyond the age that the curse of his bloodline would normally permit. I take this as a sign of his greatness."

"As do I," said Shankon, who needed no grape to prompt the correct response.

"I like The King," Granger added, but his higher pitch seemed out of the hearing range of the three adults.

"So, my husband might seal his fate in all history as The King who banished the dragons ever more. Shankon, will we be ready to defeat the dragons by nightfall tomorrow?"

"Our readiness increases by each minute," Shankon said.

"You see? That's what I told you," The King chimed in.

"But the balance can only be written in the battle," Shankon added.

And they all leaned back in their cushions to wonder what that would mean in two days' time.

"Have you had your breakfast?" Lady Thwarte asked, pulling the sash for the servants.

Chapter 31

The Ancient Draft of Authority

That afternoon, Sir Gregory sought an emergency meeting of the Assembly, but Shankon thought that would be a distraction at a crucial time. It was not as if Assembly meetings were productive events, and each member had already been assigned individual tasks that were critical to the survival of the kingdom.

"Under the Ancient Draft of Authority, I'm empowered to convene in an emergency," Sir Gregory declared.

"Not so," Shankon said. "A quorum is needed, and a quorum is denied by the urgent tasks the various members are already engaged in."

"Where do you get this theory?" Sir Gregory snapped. "From thin air?"

"From the Ancient Draft of Authority itself," Shankon said mildly. "If you doubt it, come with me and we'll put the question to Horace the Archivist."

And that was how Shankon and Sir Gregory found themselves marching shoulder to shoulder through the corridors, neither looking at the other until they arrived at Horace the Archivist's door.

Shankon dropped back half a pace and gestured to Sir Gregory who took that as permission to pound the butt of his hand against the door. "Horace!" he called out. "Step lively, man. We need your advice on a most urgent matter."

At length, Horace cracked the door and peered out through eyes large as hen's eggs at these alarming petitioners.

"Damn it, man!" Sir Gregory shouted, pushing against the door. "Let us in!"

Horace looked especially frail today. He stumbled back a step or two with the force of the door, put his right hand to his heart as if about to take an oath, then crumpled to the floor.

Shankon, who had long ago studied, but not practiced, the medical arts, knelt over Horace and searched him for vital signs.

"I'm afraid the kingdom is without an archivist," he announced, rising with some effort to his feet.

"Then I'll have to show you myself," Sir Gregory said, stooping to rip the thong holding the weighty key to the archives from Horace's neck. He rushed to the massive oak door behind Horace's body and fumbled briefly with the lock.

"It's here," he shouted. "Now you'll see!"

Sir Gregory blew dust from the folio containing the Ancient Draft of Authority, and beheld the page.

Shankon allowed him a moment, but he grew impatient himself. "Out with it," he said. "Give me your citation."

Sir Gregory placed the folio and its contents on the desk and sighed as he turned and left the room without another word. Shankon stepped up to the desk and sneezed from the dust that had been stirred up. And he saw that the paper that had prescribed every detail of the social contract, that had cramped the lives of every citizen from the lowest peasant up to The King himself, since a time long before living memory, was no more than a blank sheet.

Ever the optimist, Shankon thought that at least that was the end of Sir Gregory's emergency session.

He considered taking this revelation to The King, but ulti-mately decided that would be counter-productive at the moment. Civilization could muddle along a little bit longer, by momentum, if nothing else. Once the situation with the dragons had been resolved, they could attend to governance.

Instead, he went to the Royal Stables, borrowed a handsome bay gelding, and rode out of the castle's gates. They picked their way up the switchback to the high ridge that overlooked the castle and the city beyond.

Shankon had convinced the topiarist to send a small army of his skilled workers up here to transform the brush, and he was eager to inspect their blade work.

Chapter 32

The Battle of Topiary Ridge

It was late afternoon when a great flock of messenger birds arrived, their wings beating frantically against the sky. All of them bore the same warning: The time was at hand.

The buglers sounded in mournful waves, one after the other, passing the alert to every ear, with a force that could stir even the deaf.

Shankon sent Granger to the catacombs for safety, and rushed to take his place on the Great Parapet, just as thousands of others took up the positions they'd been assigned.

Soon enough it was obvious what had inspired the messenger birds' frenzy: A more terrible flock spilled over the horizon, their leathery wings beating in time to the foul wind of their heavy breath. They flew in so tight a formation that they brought their own nightfall, blotting the sun, and their ten thousand smoldering yellow eyes made a mockery of the stars.

Shankon saw two riders outside the castle gates, plodding under some considerable weight up the switchback he had so recently visited. Through his glass, he could make out the Archbishop and his valet, their horses laboring under bulging bags.

They were too far away to hear if he called out, and it would have been useless in any case. So Shankon watched helplessly as half a dozen of the lead dragons swooped down, almost gracefully, and with a single, perfectly orchestrated belch of fire, reduced the two men and their innocent horses to ash.

The team of marauders disappeared back into the flock, but that was when the swarm spotted the army of green dragons lining the high ridge. A large contingent broke off from the flock to investigate this manifestation, unlike anything a dragon had ever seen before.

And as they glided in close enough to inspect these abominations, somehow plants, yet somehow dragons, huge weighted nets flew out along the length of the ridge, entangling the beasts as they dropped to the bottom of the cliff, thrashing themselves against the rocks.

The soldiers rushed out of hiding with mighty cheers, rolled cauldrons of boiling oil to the edge of the cliff, and tipped the contents on the cursed enemy below.

Although the gut-churning stench and the unworldly death shrieks of the devil birds would resign a few of the men to a state resembling insanity, the plan otherwise worked just the way Shankon had described it to Granger after their visit to the topiary.

"The dragons have been improving their assaults over time because, as a species, they learn from their mistakes," Shankon had told Granger. "We learn much less efficiently, but everything mankind has learned has been the result of curiosity. So I reason that the dragons must also be curious creatures; probably even more so than ourselves."

Granger marveled at his uncle who was not his actual uncle. "How do you think this stuff up?" he wondered.

"Ah! You ask the wrong question," Shankon had said. "For you were the inspiration, when you asked me in the garden what would happen if we saw our own likenesses rendered in the shrubs. Don't you remember? You should hold that memory dear."

And years later, as Granger would indeed recount the episode, not so much as an illustration of his, or even Shankon's, brilliance, but as a study in how the human tapestry is woven one thread upon another. Although, he did come to realize that his tale, which had become a foundational legend of the New Kingdom, could win him a friend in the tavern.

When the dust cleared enough for the kingdom to appoint a new archivist, the Battle of Topiary Ridge would be hailed as the first victory in the Great Dragon War.

But wars are never settled on a single battle.

Chapter 33

The Counting of the Dead

Shankon had scant time to savor his success with the topiary dragons. That skirmish seemed to hardly diminish the greater flock which appeared to be circling the castle and city to plot their next assault.

From the Great Parapet, he turned his glass to gauge the readiness of the watchmen at the other towers that rose from the castle walls.

Shankon cursed his eyes. They'd grown so old he didn't know if he could trust them anymore. For it seemed that Sir Gregory and one of his aides had commandeered the second tower to the east. To Shankon's eye, it looked as if they were alternately brandishing, then covering their lamps in some strange sequence. Had the man gone mad? Or was he sending some kind of signal to his accomplices, or to the gathering monsters themselves? Or was Shankon himself going mad and this hallucination was merely the product of that madness?

He had little time to wonder, as a squadron of dragons dove down from their scaly ceiling and in an instant transformed the noble Sir Gregory, that pompous obstructionist and paramour of his own inglorious voice, into a cinder; his lieutenant a wisp of smoke.

It occurred—just fleetingly—to Shankon that perhaps

some good could come from even these terrible beasts. But he had no time to linger on such thoughts, and he would keep them to himself.

In any case, the direct attack on the castle—regardless of the victim's identity—was a signal to the gunners who released their first, brutal volley. The cannon balls punched holes through the damnable curtain that had cut off the sky. Many dragons were killed outright, reduced to gristle and a spray of orange blood. Others dropped in writhing heaps, where teams of assassins that Shankon had personally trained dispatched them.

"Ride my blade to Hell, you wretched demon!" was the cry Shankon had taught them to shout as their knives pierced the beasts' black, oily hearts. He'd thought of it not so much for its effect on the dragons, who despite their intelligence, surely had not mastered the native tongue, but as an inspiration for the men. And each of their cries fed off the other in a terrible chorus that would resound in the history books once a proper Archivist was appointed for the kingdom.

The battle raged for several hours until, quite abruptly, the dragons withdrew, and headed back up the valley towards the headwaters.

Night—the true night now, not the enemy's sham of a night—had fallen. Shankon sent word to Winton's team to ring the bells over the castle and the city. Normally, that authority would be reserved to the Archbishop, but no further instructions would be forthcoming from that source.

With the all-clear signal, the citizen warriors went to work. They set pyres where the dragons lay, for there was no time to gather the carcasses for a bonfire. They assessed their own casualties, and handed reports up, just as Shankon had planned.

For even in his years in the wilderness, Shankon had been planning for this day.

The messenger birds had been very concise in reporting the gathering of the dragons over recent days. A warning on a bird's leg band had no room for flowery language.

Just the same, these reports from the strategic units throughout the kingdom went right to the heart of the matter, as Shankon had designed the system to do. Human deaths. Human wounded. Dragon deaths. There was no tally of dragons wounded, nor of prisoners taken, as mercy belonged to a time long forgotten.

So the raw numbers streamed in to Shankon over the next several hours. And he presented his tally to The King.

"It seems we have thinned their numbers by nearly a thousand," Shankon said.

"Excellent!" cried The King.

"What fraction is that of all the dragons?" Lady Thwarte asked, stepping up to the side of the throne.

"We had not time for an accurate census," Shankon admitted, tipping his head. "But we have calculated that it was between ten and twenty percent of the force that attacked us today. Of course, we cannot tell if they have held other demons in reserve, or if today's assault was all they could muster."

"Right, right," The King said, clapping his hands on his armrests.

"And what of our casualties?" Lady Thwarte didn't wait for The King to calm down.

"We're still awaiting some reports," Shankon admitted. "But perhaps no more than a hundred deaths. I'm told twice that many have significant injuries, but a third of those should be battle worthy within a week."

"Excellent, excellent," The King said.

"Won't a week be too late to matter?" Lady Thwarte asked.

"Possibly," Shankon conceded. "But in whatever tongue they use, these are the same questions the dragons are asking themselves tonight. And the raw numbers show us in ascendance."

Normally a page would have escorted Shankon back to his quarters, but tonight even the youngsters were diverted from their routines to aid the war effort. It little mattered, for Shankon knew the way well enough, but he was surprised to hear his name when he made a turn in the corridor.

"Shankon!"

He pulled up short and looked back to see Lady Thwarte hurrying behind him.

"Your Ladyship—?"

"Come over here." Lady Thwarte glanced around but the corridor was empty as she tugged Shankon's arm to bring him into an alcove that looked out over the dark courtyard.

"How can I be of service, Your Ladyship?" Shankon was puzzled, a state he did not enjoy.

"The King seeks a more active role," she said, barely breaking a whisper.

"As The King, he guides our every move. How could he be more active than that?"

"But he's sequestered while history is written around him." Her eyes searched Shankon's for understanding. "He doesn't need to throw a spear—and we don't need that spectacle. But perhaps he could come out to at least bear witness to the battle?"

Shankon wondered where this concept had come from, and where he should steer it.

"Even when we hold the advantage, a dragon might strike without warning and turn the game," Shankon tried to explain, without confidence that his argument was landing. "With the medical frailties of The King's lineage, even a small wound could prove mortal.

"And besides, throughout history, the monarch has been too valuable to risk near the battlefield. Perhaps Your

Ladyship might soothe his restless temper?"

Her green eyes flashed at Shankon. "So, you would imprison The King against his will?"

"The times are fraught with danger," he countered. "How much worse if the people were to lose The King through mis-adventure in the midst of this threat?"

Lady Thwarte softened by measures. "Shankon, you know better than most that he is a fool..."

"He is My King," Shankon stopped her. "But like all of us, he shares in mankind's lot."

"And you know that he is very fragile—apart from his weak blood," she said. "Affirmation sustains him, and if the Archbishop or Sir Gregory had survived this day, I think they would have provided quite different counsel than yours."

"Which is precisely my point, Your Ladyship. If those two had taken my advice to heart, they might still be providing their counsel to The King." Shankon spread his hands and shrugged. But he saw no sorrow in Lady Thwarte's features in regards to the Archbishop and the politician. In fact, her mood seemed to improve.

"But he can be willful, Shankon," she added. "And if The King makes his way to your side, he will be yours to look after."

She waved him away, and Shankon continued on to his apartment, perhaps a little more slowly than before. And he strained to remember a time when The King, always the out-spoken sovereign, would have been reluctant to bring a request like this to Shankon in person.

Chapter 34

Scenes from a Life

When he returned to the apartment, Shankon was unconcerned by Granger's absence. He was just a boy, but he kept his wits about him. No doubt Winton had enlisted him to help with his team's tasks.

Although the hour grew late, Shankon didn't feel tired, or perhaps he felt too tired to sleep, which amounted to the same thing. So he pulled a chair from the table, with the stuttering scrape of wood against the stone floor. And he clasped his hands, and pressed them to his forehead like a man in prayer, although he beseeched no deity.

Shankon called back the years in a series of vignettes with no particular order to them. In his mind, he saw himself boarding the great boat for his first trip abroad. The faces of beggars with whom he'd shared broth and bread—as well as those of kings and great scholars—passed before him without discrimination.

He saw the highlights and low points of his life, along with events that seemed of little consequence. That was how he thought of his introduction to The Old King—who was the father of the present monarch—and of the tragedy of Granger the Elder and Geneva. Those images bookended a memory of Shankon, barely old enough to walk unassisted, stumbling barefoot after a chicken that clucked in alarm and seemed no more agile than himself.

Funny things, these memories of one's life. But what else were you left with when the bells were about to chime?

The door opened and Granger slipped in, seeming startled to find Shankon at the table in the flicker of a half-spent candle.

"We were rolling bandages," Granger said. "Winton and me and some of the others."

"And that's a good job." Shankon lowered his hands and nodded, gradually arriving back in the apartment from a distant shore. "You should get your sleep before morning."

"I'm not really tired." Granger took the chair opposite Shankon.

"It's good to be wakeful and eager for the day," Shankon conceded. "But we also need the restoration of sleep."

"I can't sleep," Granger said in a voice he might use to explain it to a younger child. "And neither can you, I see."

Shankon wanted to laugh, but it manifested itself as little more than a quake of his shoulders and an embarrassed smile. His finger traced the wood grain on the table as if this were a map to a new, exotic land. Granger's eye tracked every line and arc of Shankon's gestures.

"These are important times in our lives," Shankon said after awhile. "We see that life and death are not such different things as we'd always imagined.

"A hundred of our people fell today. Do the deaths of a thousand dragons provide a balm for that pain?"

Granger looked wide-eyed at Shankon, as he often did during the old man's lectures and reveries, until he gradually realized it was not a rhetorical question.

"No, sir."

"No, indeed." Shankon licked his fingers and snuffed the candle. Granger saw the wisp of smoke rise in the moonlight that breached the window.

"No, indeed," Shankon repeated. "We've done a poor job

of leaving you a better world. We will never defeat evil, and it has taken me a long, long time to come to that confession. Yet we must learn to live and prosper despite evil's challenges. That must be our true goal. But evil always changes. It adapts to any setback, and returns anew. Mankind needs to become just as agile. Nowhere is it written that if we lose we can carry on with some reduced stature in the universe.

"No, we cannot defeat evil." Shankon's hand stopped moving over the table, but Granger barely noticed in the moonlight. "Nor will we survive its triumph."

Chapter 35

The Children's Army

Granger woke before sunrise on the longest day of his life, but Shankon was already gone. Someone had left an apple, a hunk of bread with honey and a mug of milk on the table. Everything was arranged too artfully to be Shankon's handiwork, which made Granger think of the lives of the servants, performing their tasks in some silent, invisible world.

A world that now held some allure for Granger.

He ate the bread, drank the milk, and wrapped the apple in his sash before descending to the bowels of the castle where he reunited with Winton and his cohort.

There were perhaps half a hundred of them, some a little younger than Granger, and some just shy of battle-age. Granger had seen a pair of the smiling girls, who had shaped his fond memories of Arvon's Day, and he set about his work close enough that he might overhear the melody of their voices.

Nobody needed any instruction. They all knew their tasks well enough from the last several days. And for the most part, everyone worked in silence. They rolled bandages. They filled skins with water and worked the pulleys to lift them to the ramparts. They mixed gunpowder from the dragon dung that had been collected overnight, and poured it into carts that a procession of donkeys hauled up the winding corridors to the gunners outside. They transformed hardwood dowels, some goose feathers and a wicked, bronze tip into arrows that could bring down a four-hundred-weight dragon.

Except for the low, industrial song of the tools, the cavernous room remained nearly silent. The chief exception to that rule was Freckled John, a boy with a couple of years on Granger, but lagging Granger in every other measure.

"We're like ducks on a pond here," Freckled John suddenly announced, looking up from the rip in a soldier's tunic that he had been mending. "The dragons could fly right down the chimney and kill us all for breakfast!"

Winton scowled at the boy. "A dragon couldn't squeeze through the chimney. And even if it somehow did, it couldn't fly or control its fall. It would break its neck when it landed in the fireplace. And then we would pull it out and dance on its wings!"

Freckled John fell silent as the other kids snorted and chuckled. But after sometime, when the room had been silent for a long while, he spoke up again.

"A dragon could breathe fire down the chimney and burn us all to a crisp! I've heard their breath has the strength of the ocean's gale!"

Winton raised his voice to address the entire room. "We need someone to work by the hearth in order to block any hellfire the dragons transmit through that outlet. If we have no volunteer, we will conscript the next person who speaks."

Freckled John ducked his head and doubled the pace of his repairs, and he was not heard from again that morning.

At mid-day, Granger split his apple four ways and shared the wedges with his neighbors. Maybe half the children had a piece of fruit or a heel of bread, and that proved enough for everyone to have a bite of something. The meal lasted but a few minutes, and then they returned to their work.

"They have legs!" Freckled John suddenly realized, apparently believing Winton's earlier order of silence had expired. "They don't need to fly! They could be running down the hallways, coming for us, right now!"

Without a word, Winton strode up to Freckled John, grabbed him by the collar and dragged him to the hearth.

"Work here," he said. "And don't miss your quota."

"But what if a dragon comes down the chimney, or sends his flames?"

"Would you rather work as a sentry outside the door?"

One of the girls Granger rather fancied pitched a ball of string that bounced off the side of Freckled John's head. The young workers drew some energy from the episode, and for several minutes, one child or another would break into spontaneous laughter, which incited the others.

It was late afternoon when a page burst through the door and went straight to Winton. They whispered back and forth for a bit. Granger couldn't hear what they were saying, but he knew from Winton's face that the news was not good.

The battle was not going well above them. As a precaution, they needed to move furniture against the doors, and yes, the fireplace. They had to douse the torches and lamps, and lie down in silence until they received further instructions.

"Says who?" someone shouted.

Winton turned to the page, who was accustomed to making announcements in large chambers. "By order of the Crown Prince," he said.

Even in this naïve audience, the declaration drew a collective gasp. The Crown Prince was a cipher. His existence was known, but beyond that, his age, appearance, and temperament were popular mysteries. And how had he come to be giving orders to the youngsters? Or to anyone, for that matter? What was really going on overhead?

These were the questions that this army of children contemplated in the dark, during their hours of silence which stretched deep into the night.

Many times growing up, Granger had been put to bed prematurely by Shankon, at least by Granger's reckoning. He would toss and turn, fuss and fume as if proving that it was too early for sleep. But this time, like those around him, he mulled over the strange circumstances in this silent darkness and found himself drifting off to sleep, exhausted by this strange convergence of his past and his future.

They'd lost all sense of time when they heard a fist pounding against the door.

Chapter 36

Good Tidings, Bad Tidings

When Granger and a dozen of his comrades had cleared the door, a process that took longer than barricading it had, Lawrence and Karamus, strode in, each carrying a torch. Daramus and Paramus followed closely.

Lawrence passed his torch to Winton, who went about the great room relighting the sconces and lamps, and lending his fire to others who spread the light to the farthest corners.

To Granger, it seemed that the four men had brought the smell of sweat, blood and burnt powder down here from the real world. Their sunken eyes looked out from haggard faces in the flickering wash of Karamus' torch. Whatever they'd seen in this long, miserable day had drained their color and diminished their posture.

When light had been restored throughout the room, Lawrence stepped ahead of the others and said, "It will soon be morning, and however weary we may be, we will make a full account of this awful day so that your children, and their children alike until the end of time will know what has happened here."

Lawrence took the torch from Karamus and held it over his head and raised his voice even higher. "For we repelled the enemy and little expect it to menace us again!"

A few of the children clapped, but no cries of exultation echoed off the stone walls.

With his hands free of the torch, Karamus hugged Winton to him. And Winton, who would have been embarrassed by such a thing at any other time, did not resist.

"Father," he said, "I think you need a bath."

"I would gladly jump in the moat, but it's befouled with dragon blood." He pulled Winton even tighter and choked a little, quickly clearing his throat to cover it.

Lawrence looked around the room as if he'd lost something. He put his arm around Granger and pulled him closer, though not as tightly as Karamus and Winton.

"Didn't that sound like good news?" Lawrence whispered.

"Indeed!" Granger said. "It's wonderful!"

"I'd thought your friends would give such news a better reception?" Lawrence was looking for advice.

"I think we've learned that one shouldn't raise one's hopes too high, lest the price be too great when they are dashed," Granger said, studying the deep, new lines in Lawrence's face. "At least, that's what I've learned."

Lawrence considered this and brushed his hand over his chest, as if chasing a crumb from his filthy, blood-spattered tunic, and he whispered, "I was trying to build them up to ease the sting of the bad news."

Granger just shrugged. What else could you do with adults?

Lawrence straightened himself and cleared his throat.

"While we can leave our fear behind," Lawrence said, "Not one of us will ever truly leave this day behind. For each of us has lost someone, a father or mother, a sister or brother, a dear, irreplaceable friend who fell defending that bright line that separates good from evil.

"Songs will be sung and histories written celebrating today's heroes. And I could speak ten thousand words of the bravery and valor that have allowed us to share this moment, in this dank room, on this very special night. But even a hundred thousand words would be a swindle for the price each of you has paid. The price that all of us have paid."

Lawrence closed his eyes tight and shook his head so that Granger wondered if he could carry on. But after a long break, he continued.

"The King—the only king you have known in your short lifetimes—has died," Lawrence said, his voice cracking. "And the Crown Prince is now The King."

This brought a gasp from the audience. Scattered sobs rose up as the truth of it set in.

"But The King will be a wise and benevolent ruler, in keeping with the traditions of his lineage."

Granger couldn't help but screw up his face at this. Shankon had passed on many tidbits that seemed at odds with this declaration. But Lawrence had his momentum now.

"And I vow, that as long as the kingdom shall be—which is until the end of time—" he said, "we will mark Shankon's Day as the very cornerstone of our calendar."

Lawrence yanked Granger to him so tightly that the boy's head whipped back and forth over his neck.

In his short life, Granger had often wanted to leap back in time a few, brief moments, so he could put the implications of what he'd just learned into the context they demanded. That was at least a weekly experience when Shankon would toss out one bizarre concept or another that seemed to under-mine everything he had known about everything.

And now Shankon's Day was going to supplant Arvon's Day. Yet Arvon's Day did not exist before Arvon's death.

Granger's head spun faster than the carousel he'd ridden at the last Arvon's Day festival.

And only Karamus, quick-tempered Karamus, was swift enough to push away his own son and catch Granger's head before it cracked against the stone floor.

Chapter 37

What Happened Above

Granger's eyes fluttered open. Where was he? Why were Karamus and a host of his friends waving fans over his face? It all came back to him quickly, and his head fell against the cushion of Karamus' hand.

"Your uncle saved my life," Karamus said.

"He was not my uncle," Granger said.

"Well whoever the old fool was, he saved my life. Not once, but twice."

Winton and a few of the others would tell Granger later that his eyes seemed glazed and that his wits appeared to be in retreat.

For his own part, Granger distinctly remembered looking up past Karamus, Lawrence, Winton and the other faces to the curve of the ceiling. He marveled at the beauty of the intricate silver filigree that decorated a surface so seldom appreciated. Or was that just random scallops in the plaster, left by careless workmen?

With everyone pressing around him, Granger gagged himself into a coughing fit.

"Give him air!" Lawrence shouted. "He needs some space!"

Karamus helped him sit until the coughing subsided. Granger looked around and regained some presence.

"You probably want to know what happened," Karamus said.

In fact, Granger wasn't sure that he did want to know, but he was still too disoriented to convey that to Karamus.

"Twice saved by your uncle," Karamus said, soldiering on. "I heard him call my name and looked up just in time to avoid a wounded dragon that fell from the sky, not a sword's length from my boots.

"You could see that his bones were crushed. His left wing was folded back unto itself. His breast sported pockets that a large dog could hide in, and his legs looked like he found them. His blood spilled out with the color and stench of a rotting pumpkin. There was a glaze to his eye and I knew he wouldn't last long, but he still had his fire. So as he was turning his head to burn one of my men, I saw my opening. And because of Shankon, I knew just where to thrust my dagger. I carved out its liver and we fed it to the swine!

"That was the first time your uncle saved my life."

Granger nodded, too tired to press the point about genealogy.

"The second time was when a curtain of a hundred or more demon-birds swooped towards us with not an inch between their wingtips. You know that awful whistle of an arrow grazing your ear?" Karamus looked into Granger's eyes and realized the boy probably had never experienced such a thing.

"Well, that times a thousand might match the banshee cries raining down on us. Shankon answered them with a perfectly timed volley of the cannons and the whole chain crashed to earth, either their entrails blown out by the cannon balls, or knocked senseless in the tangle where they could be quickly dispatched. The blood flowed over our knees as we ripped out their organs and hoisted them on pikes above the watchtowers."

The story laid out by Karamus had been delayed here and there by gasps and wild cheers, and a great deal of applause. So by now, Granger had worked up the strength and focus to ask, "And Shankon?" although his voice quavered.

Karamus lifted his head, and it seemed to pull him into a standing position where he offered his hand to help Granger from the floor. Karamus looked in turn to Daramus and Paramus, who shied from his gaze.

Lawrence cleared his throat and rested a hand on Granger's shoulder.

"Nobody winced at Shankon's parables and riddles and awkward songs more than I," Lawrence admitted. "But the only one who could properly tell his story would have been Shankon himself. He dwelt upon a different plane than the rest of us, and though we mocked him with our mud-bound feet, and cringed when he poked fun at our manners, and plugged our ears at the ill melodies of his songs—oh, God forgive him those songs—still we listened and understood that we could learn in our listening."

It was quite warm in the great room from being shuttered for so long. Lawrence doffed his helmet and wiped his sleeve over his face and brow, as if brushing back the sweat, but Granger saw that the motion also blotted away some tears.

Lawrence took several deep breaths and continued.

"So forgive me this pale narration." He drew two more long, ragged breaths, searching for his words. "By right, by custom and by expectation, there was no need for The King to visit the Great Parapet at a time so fraught with danger. But visit he did for that was the sort of King he was. And while peril soared in every corner of the sky, The King took the measure of the battle. He saw the foul residue of the winged hordes seeping out to poison our fields and the grounds of our cities. And he wept for our own fallen people."

Around the room, many were snorting against sobs.

Karamus, Daramus and Paramus hung their heads. Even Granger, who was the only one who had actually met The King, and was therefore insulated from the common fantasy, felt his breath catch.

"And in this unguarded moment, the Cohort of the Seven, the most deadly dragons of all, detached themselves from that awful umbrella over the castle and dove for the Great Parapet.

"Did the monsters even know who their target was? Who can say? And does it even matter now? The catapults sent two of them to their reward before they could strike. But as Shankon saw the remaining five closing in at frightful speed, he dove for The King to cover his body with his own.

"Those five dragons blasted the Great Parapet with flames unseen outside of Hades. Shankon, and every other man standing watch, succumbed, save The King."

Lawrence needed quite some time to pull himself up before going on.

"Shankon had taught us warriors a technique whereby a man of just a hundred forty pounds could defeat a four-hundred pound, thrashing, fire-breathing dragon with a dagger that slipped between its protective plates directly into its shriveled, pungent heart. 'Shank them,' is how we exhort each other."

Now Lawrence paused because Karamus, Daramus and Paramus began weeping openly. But the story had to be told.

"So, while Shankon and the other soldiers were consumed by the flame, The King survived due to the cover Shankon gave him."

Lawrence cast his gaze at the children around the room, and let issue tears like his brother.

"You are probably too young to know the ironies of fate, and I pray that you will never know a crueler twist than this."

Karamus, Daramus and Paramus nodded their heads

deeply, like horses at feeding time, for they knew what was next.

"Shankon's dagger was drawn when he fell upon The King to protect him, and the blade grazed the royal thigh. Truly, it was a minor wound, barely a scratch, to be shrugged off by you or I. But for someone of The King's constitution, it proved catastrophic.

"The King served longer than any of his own ancestors. And now the Crown Prince will pick up that mantle. Long live The King!"

There was a long pause as the children struggled to absorb all this.

And then they shouted, "Long live The King!"

Chapter 38

A World of Fresh Orphans

Although the danger had passed, those were busy days at the castle and the city below. The King was crowned and he addressed the throng from the balcony, with Lady Thwarte's hand resting lightly on his shoulder.

Granger had never seen anyone so young wearing the diadem, yet the pale-skinned monarch showed no discomfort. He spoke of hope and optimism and renewal. The crowd cheered in all the right places, and ten minutes after his conclusion, no one could remember a word of it.

For the most part, the people were too busy to dwell on platitudes. Perhaps a third of the population awaited burial. The heavy carcasses of dragons needed to be dragged to pits and set afire. Buildings needed restoration as much from cannons and catapults that had missed their mark as from the hellish breath of the invaders. The very soul of the kingdom yearned for a healing touch.

Lawrence, Karamus and a few other soldiers led expeditions into the countryside to search out and destroy any dragons that had escaped their just fate.

On the third evening, a page came to the apartment and declared, "Lady Thwarte desires a word."

He bowed and backed out of the room as Lady Thwarte herself entered. "Poor Granger!" she said, but not coming closer than the first steps she'd taken through the door. "Who would have imagined that our griefs would merge into one?"

Granger hadn't come to terms with his own grief, but judging by its weight on his heart, he thought Lady Thwarte seemed to have come through hers at a lighter cost. But maybe that was the benefit of being an adult. He would have liked to take up the discussion with Shankon, but of course, he couldn't.

She took a few tentative steps closer, and the tips of her fingers caressed the corner of the table.

Before this, Granger hadn't noticed the startling green beauty of her eyes. Perhaps he hadn't been this close to her before, and surely she had never given him enough attention for him to catch them as he did now.

"Will you remain here?" here right arm swept the room, even as the tips of her left fingers remained on the table. "Which you are most welcome to do for as long as you please. Or do you have other plans? Perhaps to go abroad?"

Granger had no idea how he would go abroad even if that was somehow a goal he had harbored. When he'd talked with his peers, a question was a question and it received an answer on its merits. When he'd talked with Shankon, a question might be a question, or it might be a flag planted on a hill for opposing views to fight over.

But this conversation seemed like something else again. Did she want him to leave? Then why? And if she put it to him as a question, did that mean she did not have the power to make it happen? And if that was the case, did that mean that he had some undiscovered power himself?

It was all too much for one of Granger's age. Or it would have been except that his mind's eye and ear conjured a manifestation of Shankon, offering him the words he needed, like a bowl of plums, fresh from the tree at their old home.

"Queen Mum, I understand that the membership of the

Assembly has been as decimated by the war as the general population, and that there are many vacant seats?"

Her eyebrows lifted and her hand finally left the table. "That is true. You're an amazing young man."

"Am I?"

"To keep abreast of such matters. That's uncommon for a young man of your age."

"Wouldn't The King, that is The King newly crowned, have known of such things at my age?"

"I suppose he would," she nodded, not quite wary, but beginning to lose the thread. "But that was a responsibility of his station. He would be delighted to meet you. And I could arrange that."

She winked at him, which seemed even to Granger as a most un-royal thing to do. So Granger leaned in to his momentum. "Is there an age limit to become a member of the Assembly? Or a limit for voting? I think I have enough favor among my peers to win a place representing them."

"I'm certain that you enjoy wide support," Lady Thwarte said, suppressing a smile. "But one so young as you could neither run nor vote for that office."

"Indeed?" Granger cocked an eyebrow, mimicking his apparition of Shankon. "Show me where that is written."

"Horace the Archivist handled such details," she countered, "and since he has not yet been replaced, we must rely on custom rather than written law."

"And that is because of what?"

"Because the custom is to follow custom." To Granger's eye, she looked a little flustered. "At least when there is no written precedent to the contrary."

Lady Thwarte stepped back and raised her arms to the sun streaming through the window.

"Oh my! It's such a beautiful day, and one which we deserve after all we've been through." Then she studied him for a moment. "You really take after your uncle, don't you?"

"He was not my uncle."

"But don't you agree?"

He heard the voice of Shankon in his head, an echo of a thousand lessons Granger had learned at his knee: Never agree with a gratuitous assertion for that is the wedge that leads to disaster.

"Queen Mum, I have no uncle, nor father, nor mother, nor any living relation of whom I am aware." Granger shrugged and went on, "I am an orphan in a world of fresh orphans. What are we to do? Carry on with the ways that put us in this state? Or work for something better?

"Perhaps The King newly crowned, owing to his youth and empathy, will blaze a better path for us than that older generation whose inertia led us to this crossroads. Or perhaps he will find easier ways to govern, taking bad counsel to the peril of all nations.

"But to answer your question, I shall not be lingering here. Tomorrow I will return to the home Shankon and I shared just a few weeks ago. And perhaps when I have attained a suitable age, I will return here to make what progress I can in the Assembly. Or perhaps I will go abroad, like Shankon, to see if sanity still exists in any far corner of the world."

"There's no need to be hasty," Lady Thwarte offered.

"And no need not to be," Granger said, and couldn't help but laugh.

For as long as he could remember, Shankon had plied him with proofs and theorems that slipped away as soon as they fell on his ear. But another seed Shankon planted had taken root in Granger as an exotic blend of curiosity, hope and virtue.

Whatever the intentions of Shankon and The King recently deceased, and the Archbishop, and Sir Gregory and all the rest, they'd dealt Granger's generation a poor hand. But, as Shankon himself had said, "There's no hand so bad that it cannot win."

Granger showed Lady Thwarte the door, feeling quite the adult. He went to the stables to arrange a fine gray gelding for the morning on the account of The King, and he returned to the apartment to await dinner.

In the mean time, he stood next to the table, crouched, and tried to leap upon it, but instead crashed to the floor, well short of his goal.

Granger dusted himself off and walked around the table, eying it carefully from every angle. At last, he pulled a chair out, crouched and jumped upon it, springing off of that to land in the center of the table, where he danced, spinning, until he felt dizzy.

He slept well that night. And a fine, gray gelding with the look of eagles bestowed by that great old sire, Royal Shade, was saddled and ready at dawn.